STEPHANIE VICTOIRE was born in London to a Mauritian family. In 2010 she graduated with a BA in Creative Writing from London Metropolitan University. In 2014 Stephanie completed her collection of fairy and folk tales entitled *The Other World, It Whispers* whilst on the The Almasi League writers' programme. Two of these stories were separately published in 2015. Stephanie lives in London and is currently working on a novel, *The Heart Note*.

STEPHANIE VICTOIRE

THE OTHER WORLD, IT WHISPERS

SALT

CROMER

PUBLISHED BY SALT PUBLISHING 2016

2 4 6 8 10 9 7 5 3 1

First published in Great Britain in 2016 by
Salt Publishing Ltd
12 Norwich Road, Cromer, Norfolk NR27 0AX United Kingdom

www.saltpublishing.com

Salt Publishing Limited Reg. No. 5293401

A CIP catalogue record for this book is available from the British Library

ISBN 978 1 78463 085 0 (Paperback edition)
ISBN 978 1 78463 086 7 (Electronic edition)

Typeset in Neacademia by Salt Publishing

Printed and bound in Great Britain by Clays Ltd, St Ives plc

for Norman

Contents

THE OTHER WORLD, IT WHISPERS

Time and Silence

"What would you not have accomplished if you had been free?"

- *The Count of Monte Cristo*

I SAW HER when I ran outside to dig my bleeding fingers into the snow. She was as pale as the pearl-painted landscape that ran for miles around us. If it weren't for her matted black mane, I wouldn't have noticed her. My first thought was that I had died; my mother had finally killed me and this is what the spirit realm looked like. I had found my first ghost kindred. At first she dithered back and forth between two pine trees before advancing a little towards me. I finally breathed and the cold air clouded my view for a second or two. I was not dead and she was still there. If Mother saw us there she'd chase the girl away and give me another hiding; as it was, I had abandoned scrubbing the soot from the stone hearth because I'd scraped my skin so much I couldn't hold the scourer. When I did my chores, I wasn't allowed to put on gloves or place a cushion down to save the skin on my bony knees.

The night before she'd had me cleaning the attic in the dark. "It'll test your courage, boy," she said as she descended the rickety wooden stairs and switched off the light by the door. I coughed from the dust and sweated onto the floor. I knocked a pile of things over when something ran across my hand; I didn't allow myself to imagine what it was. I fumbled to put what felt like a valise, a box of blankets and a few books back into a tower. My mother had lied about not having any spare blankets. I'd asked for an extra one for my bed when the first snow cloud rested itself above our house, a dove-coloured puff telling us that winter would be harsh and long. "We've no blankets for you. Those sheets will have to do," Mother said and slammed the door to my bedroom.

My room used to be the second bathroom just for Jenny; the oldest daughter had needed her privacy. When Jenny left home Mother said that there was no need for a second bathroom. At least I no longer had to share a room with Mindy. Mindy suffered from nightmares, and strangely, always woke up at two forty-five in the morning on the dot to scream. Mother would run in and stroke her back to sleep and scold me for just being there. "The poor thing, the poor thing, she's plagued by these terrors," Mother would coo, Mindy's sweat-sodden hair stuck to her arm. Aren't we all, I'd think to myself. But then I moved into the bathroom that was now absent of Jenny's soaps and perfumes and potions. She had left behind her lemon flannel bathrobe, which I snuck under the thin sheet on my bed just to get a little warmer. The bathtub was ripped out and so was the sink. The toilet stayed because Mother said it meant I wouldn't disturb her in the night if I woke up to go for a wee; and so there is a toilet in my room. The tiles have cracked around where the bathtub used to be. No longer supported by the grouting on the wall, they fall and thud down onto my pile of books, my six books that I cherish – they are the only things in the world that are truly mine. The librarian, Fred, gave them to me on the day Mother marched into the library and ripped me from a chair, the copy of *Robinson Crusoe* flying through the air and causing such an echo when it landed, heads turned and tutted me. I shouldn't have been at the library. I was supposed to be at the clockmakers getting our lantern clock fixed, which I had been, but Tom the clockmaker had said that it would take a few hours so I was to come back later. Well, I couldn't have gone home without the clock, so I went to the library to wait out the time. Mother dragged me out of the library and back to the clockmaker's, hissing, "Wait until it's ready," before turning on her heel to head home. Fred had watched her tugging at my scarf like she was pulling a leash on a dog, and followed us down the road.

A few minutes after Mother had left, while I was watching Tom fixing our clock and trying to avoid eye contact with me – judgment clearly rippling through his mind at what he had just witnessed – Fred poked his head through the door and handed me a bag and said nothing. He smiled at me the same way Jenny had smiled at me on the day she left home. It wasn't a joyous "don't worry about a thing" smile; it was a pitying smile, a "sorry for you" smile. Fred left quickly and I looked inside the bag. There was the copy of *Robinson Crusoe* along with *Moby Dick*, *Grimms' Fairy Tales*, *Dracula*, *The Count of Monte Cristo* and *Frankenstein*. That was the best day of my life, the greatest gift – a perfect collection. After I'd read them all, I dreamt of sailboats and wolves and monsters. The wolves and monsters were my friends and they would come and murder Mother, and the sailboat would be how Mindy and I would escape, although I don't know where the sea is. But that doesn't matter; my swordsmen and monster friends will lead us there.

I wanted more books, I wanted to add extra worlds to the six I possessed, and when I was clearing the attic in the dark and felt those familiar brick shapes, stroked their spines and smelt their musty pages, I wanted to know what stories I held in my hands. Who else would accompany us in my sailboat? I had to leave these mystery books where they were because when the light was switched on and the sound of heels pounded up the stairs, Mother immediately checked my pockets and under my shirt and in the waistline of my trousers to make sure I hadn't taken anything. "You've done an appalling job," she had said. "You'll continue this tomorrow." Then she sent me to bed.

But the girl, the wild girl, would be my saviour. We were at a stand-off outside in the cold, my fingers stinging, my blood making crimson buttons in the snow, and the clouds seeping from my mouth, cracking my lips dry. And she, with pieces of the forest in her dense, black, shaggy hair, her pale skin and her blue and purple veins surfacing on her bare chest like a map spread out on a table. She was deathly thin and dirty and I wondered how she hadn't frozen to death in what appeared to be just a slip or a nightdress. She was barefoot and her toes were the colour of charcoal. She moved closer still, but very slowly, staring at my red fingers. She must have escaped some horror out there in the forest, looking like she did. And so I asked her:

"Are you Red Riding Hood?" Perhaps she had lost her cape when grappling with the wolf. She shook her head.

"Are you Gretel?" Perhaps she'd managed to escape the witch that was trying to eat her. She got away, but her brother didn't. She shook her head again and came a bit closer.

"Who are you, then?"

"Who?" she echoed back to me, sounding like an owl. She then gasped at the sight of my fingers. "Blood," she breathed. The steam she exhaled into the biting air confirmed she was alive too.

"Yes, I hurt myself," I told her, and then she knelt down and took my hands in hers; they were not cold as I'd expected, or warm either, but still they numbed me. Her nails had lines of brown in them as if she'd been digging the earth. Her bright ice-blue eyes showed concern. Not even Jenny or Mindy had ever looked at me like that, not even on days when they might have felt bad for me, like the time Mother cut off all my hair in chunks because I'd spilled my dinner all over the floor. The plate was too hot and it had startled me when I touched it; the plate slipped and my stew splattered onto the kitchen tiles. Jenny and Mindy just watched as Mother searched for a pair of scissors, wildly telling me how useless I was while I grew desperately hungry. As I sat in the corner of our then-shared room afterwards, Mindy came and sat beside me. And instead of putting her arm around me like I'd hoped she might, she just said, "You get into trouble because you're a boy. Mummy said that boys are bad." I imagine that Jenny didn't feel this way because she married one. But then Jenny only ever got kisses and cakes from Mother so why would she dare voice her difference of opinion? There once was a time when Mindy shared her cakes with me and asked me to colour in pictures with her and begged me to read her to sleep. We haven't done these things together in a while.

"Where did you come from?" I asked the wild girl, and at this, she took her hands back and tucked them into her lap; she didn't like this question, it seemed. Just then, we both jumped at a loud *thwack* and it took a moment for me to realise that it sounded like a meat cleaver hitting a chopping board. Mother was in the kitchen and I needed to finish scrubbing: I was due to go back up to the attic soon. And then it occurred to me that I could keep the girl up there: she could hide and be with me there in the dark; she could be my friend.

"Would you like to come with me?" I asked her, and she nodded for the first time. I took her hand and led her around the house, ducking under the windows until we reached the other entrance that led us straight into the utility room, which was essentially a room designed to be used only by me. Oven trays were now clanging in the kitchen and I took the opportunity during that commotion to pull the girl up the stairs. Mindy was in the first bathroom pretending to be a mermaid, as she did for about an hour each day. She'd prepare for her bath by decorating herself in Mother's pearls and putting flowers in her hair before writhing about in the water. She could be a mermaid all she liked if we ever made it to the sea. I managed to get the wild girl and myself up to the attic without being noticed. I told the girl to sit in the corner behind the old armoire, or inside it, if she preferred. She climbed into it and I instructed her to not leave that spot until I came back to her. I said I'd be back soon and would try to bring her something to eat. "There's an evil woman in this house who won't like it one bit if she finds you. She'll punish us both. Do you understand?" She nodded again. Up there in that cramped space I could smell her: she smelt of sour milk, soil and that metallic tang that lingers on your palm when you hold coins for too long. "I must give you a name," I told her. "I need to be able to call you." She seemed to like this idea because she smiled; she had two grey canines, but otherwise her teeth weren't so bad. She waited with delight while I mulled over a few ideas. Perhaps no one had ever thought to name her before. "I'm going to call you Snow," I said finally, and she agreed, smiling wider – her eyes bluer and brighter like two globes. "OK, Snow. I will come back to you soon, I promise."

"Lucas!" My name ripped through the house in a voice so shrill I felt it vibrate in my ribs. Snow's pupils eclipsed the oceans of her irises.

"That's her, Snow. That's the evil woman." Snow tucked her knees into herself and shrunk to the back of the armoire. "I have to go."

I tore down the stairs and found Mother standing by the hearth, her black eyes locked on me. When idle they were a muted black, a misty black. When looking at me, they were fired up and shiny like polished onyx.

"Do you think you're finished here?" She pointed to the tub of sugar soap and the scourer on the floor. She looked at my blood-crusted fingers but said nothing about them.

"No, Mother," I replied. "I just went to find something to stop my bleeding. I wouldn't want to stain anything with my blood."

"You've got twenty minutes to finish this. Then up to the attic you go."

⁂

Snow helped me clean. She helped me to see in the dark, helped me find my way around the attic. Her numb, bloodless hands took the cloth, put it in my hand and guided it over the dust on the boxes, cases and other surfaces. We whispered in the black afternoon. I told her about my plan to get to a sailboat and sail far, far away. She answered with small words like, "Yes, I'll help," and even though she was a quiet thing, I knew that she understood the weight of my situation.

"But how will I escape her, Snow?" I asked. There was silence. In this silence, I wondered how long it would be before I was running free through the forest. "We have to take Mindy," I continued.

"Mindy?" she questioned; that name in her mouth sounded like the whip of a breeze.

"Yes, she's my little sister."

"Yes, I'll help," she repeated. She couldn't see my eyes begging her silhouette to make it all OK. I tucked her into the back of the armoire and she immediately started gnawing on the biscuits I had brought her. I reminded her to be dead silent when Mother came up and she stopped nibbling straight away. I imagined she was holding the biscuit in her mouth with her earthy fingers, like a squirrel ready to protect her food. The light came on and I closed the armoire doors and resumed my position on the floor with the cloth in my hand. Mother appeared, looked around and said nothing about the state of the attic, which meant that I had done a good job.

"Time you had a bath, don't you think? You stink of sweat," she said as we went down the stairs.

In the tepid bath, I lay there imagining what the sea smelt like. In stories they said it was salty and they gave it all sorts of colours like marine, azure, navy, aqua and emerald. They said it was big – vast, even; I wondered just how small I'd feel against it. As I thought of names for the boat, a scream tore through the house, which was followed by a quick series of thumps. I panicked – I was sure Mother had found Snow. I jumped out of the bath and threw my dusty clothes back on, even though I was dripping wet.

"Mummy!" I heard Mindy cry. And there they both were, Mother at the bottom of the stairs on her back and Mindy crouched over her, checking her for scrapes. "What happened, Mummy?" Mindy asked frantically.

"Open the door! Open the door, Mindy!"

Mother had been walking down the stairs when she said she saw a girl through the pane of glass on the front door and the fright of it had caused her to lose her footing. Mindy opened the door and showed her that no one was there.

"There was someone there!" Mother insisted, as if it was Mindy's fault the girl had gone. Mindy was frightened by Mother's tone, perhaps because it was the first time a scolding was ever directed at her. I watched this all from halfway up the stairs and said nothing. Mother gathered herself up and stepped out of the house to look around. "I saw her," I heard her say under her breath. I'd never seen Mother that pale; I was comforted by that.

"Get me a glass of water, Lucas." Her voice quivered a little. I went to the kitchen and poured her a glass of water.

All the while I was smiling. *Well done, Snow,* I thought to myself.

Over the next few days we heard Mother scream out often and I no longer worried about Snow getting caught. She was excellent at being a ghost, and after the third time she appeared to Mother in a wisp-thin apparition like she was from some unknown, dark world, Mother stopped saying that she'd seen a girl. Mother was keeping certain words in her mouth; you could almost see them, like they were made up of Scrabble tiles that spelled out "I think I'm being haunted." They piled up behind her lips, jumbled on her tongue. After she fell down the stairs that day, she sat in the armchair in the living room with her feet up on the footstool, sipping her water and hoping that Mindy and I would vanish so that we wouldn't see the terror all tangled up around her nerves – but I could see her desperately trying to steady her hands. Once she'd composed herself she soon found a chore that she could order me to get on with.

"Lucas, go and sweep the snow off the path outside. It's piled up out there," she said with her eyes locked on our now-working lantern clock. As I stepped out of the house holding the shovel with my gloved hand, I looked up at the attic window and I saw Snow standing there, waving at me. I couldn't see her smile, but I imagined she was smiling at me, pleased with our first victory over my mother. And through the window like that she did look like a ghost; or perhaps she was actually an angel, because just in that moment snowflakes started to fall from the sky as if it was her who had made it rain tiny white feathers, just for me.

The next night Mother's screech came from the bathroom. I don't know how Snow pulled this one off, but she'd appeared to Mother through the screen door of the shower cubicle. Mother must have been in there, burning away the day in a hot shower, soaped up and basking in the steam, when she caught sight of Snow in the room, watching her through the haze. Mother screamed and slipped, but managed to catch herself, although she said she had banged her elbow. Before she could wipe away the steam, switch the water off or step out of the cubicle, Snow had vanished. I knew she had run back up to the attic without a sound, the way a mouse gets back into a hole in the wall. I never heard her footsteps, even though I listened out for her: not a creak she made. When Mother came out with a towel around her, her elbow red and her face puffed with steam, she was shouting, "Where are you?! Where are you?!" She woke up Mindy, who came out of her bedroom in her Winnie the Pooh nightie, weeping and rubbing her sleepy eyes. I had been lying on my bed, picking at the remaining tiles on the wall with one hand and holding my copy of *Frankenstein* in the other, thinking about just how much I liked the voice of the monster and how he didn't frighten me at all. I knew not to run out to her. I took my time, set my book down and prepared myself for playing dumb.

"Who are you talking to, Mother?" I asked, examining her face and noticing how much she looked like a terrified rabbit, her eyes large, her face twitching – searching left and right for a trace of the threat she was convinced was upon her.

"You're scaring me, Mummy," Mindy sobbed. Mother

didn't answer us but continued to shout at the walls. I took Mindy's hand and led her downstairs to the kitchen to get her some hot chocolate. I was never allowed any, but on this occasion I thought I could take the liberty.

Mother took herself up to bed and, for the first time ever, she didn't wake me up the next morning. It seemed she was still asleep, or perhaps just laying there awake with fear, when I tiptoed past her bedroom to take a bottle of fresh water and a piece of bread up to Snow. I tried to mimic how Snow had moved, so stealthy and silent; I worked on making my steps as light as possible. Snow seemed happy to see me, even though I couldn't see her because turning on the light might have roused Mother. But I was sure I saw her teeth glint briefly like the twinkle of a star.

"It's working, Snow. She's frightened. I know she is. But now what? What do we do?"

"Just wait," was all that her wispy voice said. And I knew that waiting was all that I really could do. Snow waited out the rest of the day and that night. She knew not to strike too often. It was almost like she could sense when Mother had untangled her nerves and resumed as normal before making another attack.

The next morning, Snow caused Mother to slice her own finger with a knife. She had been chopping apples by the window in the kitchen, intending to bake a pie. The window looks out onto the forest, which encircles the back of the house, and Mother happened to glance up and see Snow standing there between the trees. Startled and bleeding, Mother reached for a cloth, and when she looked back up again, Snow had disappeared. I watched it all happen because I was behind Mother, sweeping the kitchen floor.

"Are you all right, Mother?" I did my courtesy questioning. She didn't answer me. Mother no longer had the breath to hiss at me, no longer had the mind to watch my every move. She had stopped paying attention to me completely, and I was enjoying that. I finally had a chance to watch her, to see her quiver – see her come undone.

Later on that day I caught her whispering to herself as she sat in the living room, staring at the fire as if she was reciting a chant to conjure up fire spirits. She even stopped getting dressed in the days that followed. She'd glide around the house in her frayed, peach-coloured dressing gown, her hair no longer neatly curled and coiffed but kinked and distressed. She jumped often, even at just the sound of Mindy entering the room, whom she now looked at sideways. Her shiny onyx eyes were perishing. She no longer looked at me at all. The chores were left; all the tedious tasks I was made to perform day in and day out weren't being monitored anymore, so I stopped doing them. The banisters grew dusty, the mirrors didn't sparkle and my bed remained dishevelled. I even managed to head to town and back without a beating upon my return. I went back to the library and bid Fred a good day. He seemed surprised to see me in such high spirits, so he watched me for a while, his mouth slightly agape. I was looking for another story, something that would give me an idea of where we'd go once we were aboard the boat. I wondered what it would be like to make it to an Arabian desert, or how we'd fare living out our days in an Indian jungle. Could we be happy on a deserted island, Mindy, Snow, and me?

By the time I got home, winter seemed to have turned to spring in one afternoon. The pines peeked green hats out from the top of their snow coats; the roads had thinned to a wet glaze; grass poked through the white blankets that had kept their heads down in slumber for months, and I no longer saw my breath cloud before me. And just as winter was receding, so was the life I had always known.

When I visited Snow that afternoon, she was cradling one of the books in the attic. She wasn't reading it but rather feeling the pages with her bony fingers, with a look on her face that told me she was dreaming, just like I did when I felt the stories pour out from books and into me. We didn't talk much, but she kept assuring me that we would get away. I left her with a cup of warm milk and some toasted bread.

The house was quiet that night. Mindy had fallen asleep on the sofa and Mother was sitting in front of the fire again. I couldn't sleep, so I sat in the kitchen drawing swords and armour on the back of an old letter. I heard the crackles of the flame coming from the living room and the ticks of the lantern clock marking the silence of every passing second. And then Mother stabbed the air with another scream, making Mindy howl in response. Mother wailed and cried, "Go away!" and when I went into the living room, there was Snow standing behind Mother's chair, her reflection gazing at her through the mirror above the mantelpiece. Mother saw me appear behind Snow, and as Mother rose from her chair to confirm what she was seeing, she clutched at her chest and her arm went limp.

Mindy ran to her and I stood there not knowing what to do. And Snow didn't move either, and we watched my mother cry and Mindy cry and the panic of that moment made the fire roar. Mother was having a heart attack. Two of her fingers were twitching and her eyes looked like black buttons about to pop. Her right shoulder dropped and her earrings swung as she convulsed.

"You!" The word was a whisper, but I'm sure it was meant to be serrated like a knife. Mother panted and clutched her chest some more and bore a stare into me. "You evil! Evil!" The words flew at me out from between her clenched teeth. Mindy cried at Snow to go away but I believe those words were also meant for me.

"Mindy, let's go!" I reached for her hand but she smacked it away.

"She needs the hospital!" Mindy sobbed.

Snow pulled on my sleeve for us to go.

"Get out!" Mother collapsed down into the chair and I knew then that I could never stay.

"Mindy, come with us!" I tried one more time, but she mimicked Mother's dark venomous voice and called me evil. Mindy would never forgive me for this and she would always love Mother more; I had to leave her.

Snow bolted out of the room and I called after her, but when I got to the hallway, the front door was open; she had got away. I couldn't take Mindy, but I ran up to my room for the suitcase I had kept ready and waiting underneath my bed. I forced my feet into my shoes and lifted my coat off the rack. Before I left the house, I looked back at Mindy and Mother through the living room doorway one more time: Mother was curling into a ball in pain and Mindy shouted "murderer!" at me over and over again. And then the clock struck twelve. I felt that deathly tick of midnight like an anchor in my gut and I ran as fast as I could. Slipping on melting snow and holding my arms out to sense my way through the dark, I headed in the direction I thought Snow had gone.

As the forest deepened and the treetops blotted out the sky like a woven nest above me, I caught a glimpse of a nightdress up ahead – she had waited for me. When I reached her, she took my hand and pulled me along. I wasn't cold and I was trying not to be scared. I heard movement in the grass some distance away and the dark greens of the forest were now indigo and blurry, pierced with jagged black spikes which must have been the tree branches. I wanted to keep up all the way to wherever we got to next, but I was suddenly worried that my legs were not strong enough. I looked up at the moon for some comfort; a piece of light that would always be there. All I had left behind was gone to me now; Mother and Mindy had each other and I now saw that's all they needed. I wanted to give my baby sister a different life, but in the end, she didn't want it.

As for me, there'd be new lands and the sea, and that thought got me excited. I only looked back once to see the small glow of light from the house disappear behind the arms of the trees. Snow tugged my arm, urging me on. There was no way I could let go of her now. I looked up one more time at the moon before moving quicker, because it was then I was sure I heard the howling of a wolf.

Shanty

I SING TO the sea of my labours. I sing to its rhythm, to the gliding and swishing and the sounds it makes, like a crisp sheet of paper being slid across another, like a brush sweeping carefully through long, silky hair. I call out to the water itself, the element of intuition and the divine feminine, of fluidity and cycles, a body that responds to the moon when it is bright and full, bowing low to the earth and praising high to the sky – a worshipper at its goddess's feet. And yet so ferocious it can be, the mighty sea. It can growl and grumble and destroy. It keeps secrets from us, keeps the dark depths unknown and unseen, like a bear sitting over its young – do not upset it, it will engulf you whole. This danger to me is the ultimate masculine; after all, it has always been a man's business to battle the seas, to try to control it, to use it and to manipulate it as he has sailed across it in ships. I imagine old sailors clinking their tankards in cheer, drinks as rewards for their bravery, friendships only men at sea could forge: just them and their determination to take on the great big blue.

Blue. The colour assigned to me before I left my mother's womb. A colour forced upon boys through Babygros, blankets and toys. Blue is the colour of the tricycle I wasn't sure I wanted because the only other colour in the shop was pink and that was never an option. Blue was the colour of my first pair of trainers that my father hoped would make me sporty.

Blue was the colour of my bedroom walls that stared at me so coldly from all four sides and threatened to push my pretty posters down onto the floor. Blue was the colour of the bruises I punched into myself for being given the wrong body. Pink is the colour of the penis I look down at and despise.

I sit on the sand and shiver from the cold; it is an early spring evening when no one wants to be on the beach and so I am here alone. This is exactly where I need to be. Even though it has been raining and the sand is damp, I enjoy feeling it with my bare feet. The sand will get into my jeans and in the creases of me and will dust the ground as I walk home tonight, but I don't mind. The chill gets into the back of my collar and I pull my jacket up higher. I think that even if it was a glorious summer's day, if it was warm and comfortable, I still couldn't wear what I wish to. I am envious of women's dresses, how beautiful they must feel, how free their legs dance under swirling skirts. How their breastbones are on show and splay out across their chests, like wings made of bone, their breasts neatly cradled in a bikini top underneath. They have sleek arms that a man can wrap his whole hand around. How chunky and clumsy my hands feel. Even when I need to release some sexual frustration through this organ that won't let me forget its existence, the hand that works on it feels fat, rough and unnatural. I must apply my hand cream every hour or so just to get close to the softness I want them to possess. It is lavender-and-lemon-balm scented and I cup my hands sometimes to my nose and breathe it in; I wish to perfume myself with this fragrance. Once I spritzed a decadently floral fragrance onto my neck and it made me feel wonderful, catching wafts of myself smelling like a rose garden on a spring morning. My father crumpled his face when he caught it in the air next to me. He didn't say anything about it. I see that disgusted expression on his face often enough, when I've curled my long floppy hair with my mother's hair tongs, or worn eyeliner to see if it suited my green eyes.

Sometimes the sea is green, like the Mediterranean. Green is a neutral colour, the balance of the rainbow, the absolute middle of everything, neither masculine nor feminine, nature in its most organic state. That's the eye colour I was assigned – the in-between. I like them, I really do, but I study them in my bedroom mirror and think that they could look truly amazing if my eyelids and lashes were decorated. But then I wonder: Would a man ever look into them and think so? If I could sing the songs of the sirens in the deep waters, call up to men in their boats and lure them into my spell, then I would never have to worry about whether or not anyone would ever fall in love with me.

I found a book about mermaids and sirens and those enchant-ing creatures of the sea in a second-hand bookshop, which I usually go to at the end of my walk along the seafront parade. Some of the books are outside, stacked in crates that rest on rickety tables and their pages smell of wood and salt like driftwood. I found this book inside at the far back of the pokey shop in a pile that was sitting on the floor rather than on a shelf, between old editions of *Treasure Island* and *The Snow Queen*. The green cloth-bound cover was coming away from the spine so I had to be careful to free it from its trap.

The pages crinkled as I turned them slowly over, absorbing the words that seemed to be calling to me in the silence of that shop. At the back of the book I found a written spell in cursive blue ink and I quickly took it to the counter, which was an old desk buried under more unsorted books. The owner smiled and reached out to take the book I had chosen. She has owned this shop for decades and is going blind, but she knows exactly where all her books are and the prices of them without having to read the little pencilled numbers on the inside of every cover. I have seen her hobble slowly over to the nook under the stairs of her shop to retrieve a Japanese poetry book a customer had requested. She scanned the pile with her wrinkly fingers and knew which one she wanted by touch. I handed her my *Magic of the Sea* gently and the pearlescent glaze over her blue eyes seemed to sparkle. "This one is a real treasure," she said, whispering as if not to disturb the creatures that lay within the pages. "I fell in love with it straight away," I replied in a voice that wasn't really my own. It fell out deep, heavy and flat and thudded onto the counter like one of those books. I've often stroked my Adam's apple and wondered what would happen if I punched it in: I'd probably lose my voice. How would the mermaids hear me if I couldn't sing to them?

I hated when my vocal cords were testing out tones and pitch around the ages of twelve and thirteen and in the end settled on this one. How cruel that time was to me. I watched the school shirts of my female friends swell as their breasts grew in and their hips began to sashay down the halls instead of trudge. I would go home and stuff two balled-up socks under my shirt and stroke them over the fabric with my hands, just feeling the curves of them. It made my chest feel warm to do that, and I would hug myself and hold them tight against me, feeling a love for myself that I'd never felt before flowing back into me through that hug. As I got a little older and the appendage between my legs grew longer and more powerful, I distressed over how to make it feel like it wasn't there. I'd squash it tight into my pants, but the material would always betray me and awaken it. It throbbed in defiance and wanted me to use it. Sometimes when I was certain that no one was home, I would take off my underwear and kneel on my bedroom floor with my legs apart and imagine that there was a hole there where I am blocked. I wondered if women felt the air move through them when their legs were parted like this, the way the sea breeze moves through my skin now and tickles the fine hairs on my face.

At the age of sixteen I listened to the boys around me tease each other about their chin fluff and tell each other to start shaving so that the hairs would grow through darker and thicker. I despaired at those little whiskers making a bigger fool of me, while the acne on girls cleared away to reveal smooth, dewy skin that glowed like the figures in a Botticelli painting. I didn't want to shave, but I knew that I had to otherwise I'd be teased too, and within days the hairs grew in fast like weeds around a gravestone. My dad thought that it had been my first time using a razor and it was the only time I saw pride in his face: his son was becoming a man, no matter how much this kid tried to resist it. He had nature to thank for that. He handed me his shaving cream and stood against the door frame of the bathroom, instructing me occasionally so that I wouldn't cut myself.

But that hadn't been the first time I had used a razor. When I was fourteen, I used my mother's razor to shave my legs and I spent the rest of the evening sliding my legs up and down each other, a rush of pleasure soaring through me with every stroke. They were silky, and in the mirror they finally looked pretty. One evening, when my mum came in to say goodnight, she sat on the edge of my bed and placed a hand on my leg as she spoke. When she bid me good dreams, she rubbed it and my pyjama leg lifted to reveal my creamy, hairless skin. She said nothing, but the next morning her razor was nowhere to be seen. She had hidden it from me. And just as I had predicted, the sickness in me grew back darker and thicker with that stubble.

I am seventeen now. I still have time to undo the horrible curse that was put upon me the moment I was conceived. The moment my parents' seeds decided what sex I was to be. I am still young, and thankfully still skinny and that will do me well, keeping such horrible masculine bulks away. I won't bulge through my clothes and feel heavy when I walk like a burly giant, so vulgar this image is to me.

I've been watching the moon wax over the last week since I bought my *Magic of the Sea*. I devoured the book in half a day. I didn't go home as I usually would after my walk back from the bookshop, but came back to sit here on the beach almost in the exact same spot I am in now. And with the turn of each of those yellowed, stiff pages, I thought I could feel the presence of the mermaids and sirens grow stronger and stronger around me. I would look out to the far waters and concentrate, hoping that I had the gift of being able to see them. Some people do, like those who catch fairies shooting across the woods like tiny little fireworks, or those who can see sprites leaping over rivers like skimming stones that haven't been thrown. I read that the sirens killed sailors: they would drag them down into the deep with them as if they were collecting dolls. But mermaids, those gorgeous, alluring creatures with their perfect female torsos, their angelic faces and their lustrous hair – I wish I'd been created so. Imagine being that magnificent, that magnetic and that ethereal and with no sexual organs to complicate things. Just a tail that allows you to soar and pirouette, like a ribbon being twirled in the air by an acrobat, but in pure, blissful freedom. If I were a mermaid I'd comb my long hair a thousand times a day, sit up on the rocks and feel the sun on my glistening mermaid skin. The goddess is full tonight and the tide is rejoicing in worship. This is when the spell is to be done, when the moon is full and the waters are mighty. The mermaids have the power to transform me; they can cast the divine feminine upon me. Perhaps if I sing this shanty, the sirens will come too and drag me into the water and kill off the man in me.

Layla and the Axe

LAYLA TRUDGES THROUGH the grass across the meadow towards the forest, with Rowan by her side and the axe weighing heavy in her hands. "He won't get me. He won't get me," she mutters to herself over and over like a chant. She swats away a fly without looking at it. The height of summer buzzes all around her in the stiff heat that renders birds, bees and butterflies restless. Rowan trots along, his brush hanging low behind him, his thin legs keeping up with his friend's.

The axe that Layla carries is not clean and isn't new; it has cracked its way through logs and it has threatened a wife who didn't know how to stop her mouth. It has sat in the corner by the hearth, watching a chubby white cat writhe on the fraying rug and young, excitable girls spill tea on the sofa. It has seen snow being stamped off heavy boots and a mother sob hearty tears when the rest of the house was sleeping. And now this axe might very well be a hero. Layla has a small bruise forming on her knee from where she buckled over the locked gate and landed awkwardly and hard onto the gravel before the pale greens and dry yellows of the meadow's floor began. She had brushed herself down and waited for Rowan to squeeze through the gap, tucking his body in and making himself flat. His ears warn Layla of sounds she has yet to hear. One of his ears was scraped and scabby when she first found him.

"You're my fox now, aren't you?" she'd said softly, dabbing

hot lavender water over the injured ear with a flannel, the fragrant steam rising from the bowl and dampening her skin. Rowan, who was just called "Fox" then, was shaking and contemplating whether he should stay or bolt through the kitchen door and back through the hole in the garden where he came from. "You're my fox now. You chose me." Layla was prepared for the telling off she knew she was in for when Pa got home.

"Get that thing out of here! Do you know what diseases they carry?" Pa yelled when he came into the kitchen and saw the woodland animal shifting nervously in Layla's embrace. Pa was tall and broad – a giant even – but Layla knew that even the smallest of creatures could stand up to a giant.

The trees now appear plentiful and stretch their branches up high. Layla thinks of Alice watching the room grow tall around her. "Drink me," she says aloud, neither to herself nor to Rowan. Her mouth pushes out words to take her mind off the heaviness in her grasp.

He got to Sylvia in the spring, this monster in the forest. With her cardigan torn and a smudge of soil on her cheek, she ran straight to her mother, who now bolts her front door at sundown. "He kissed me," Sylvia whispered to Layla when they met one morning under the birch tree. "He gave me biscuits and buns and a mug of hot tea."

Rowan tucked his wiry tail in and curled up at Layla's feet.

"So why are you crying if he gave you such treats?" Layla asked, her stomach now grumbling for the blueberry pie Ma sometimes made.

"Because he kissed me, Layla. He kissed me and his fingers crept up my thigh." Sylvia had escaped with a kick to his knee and tugged her cardigan until it slipped from his clammy hand. She fell in the dirt just outside his house and thought for sure she'd never make it home.

"Who is he?" Layla asked, not sure if Sylvia was telling the truth. Layla had known everyone who'd lived in the village all the thirteen years of her life and had been going into the forest since she was seven and not once had she seen a tiny cottage anywhere in there, let alone a man who lived inside it.

But Layla and everyone else in the village believed it enough when Melody, Mrs Hanigan's daughter, hadn't been so lucky on Midsummer's Eve. It had started out as a delightful cele-bration. Everyone was gathered outside except for Sylvia and her mother, who'd closed their curtains and locked themselves in for the night. The grown-ups were merry on cider and Mr Finn made a fire pit. Rowan skittered away from it at first, until Layla began to dance around the flames with her sister, Allie, and soon Rowan looked like he was dancing too, hopping back and forth between the two girls, his orange tail puffing out in excitement. "See if you can spot the faeries, girls," Mrs Hanigan said to all the daughters. Her cheeks were rosy with cheer. She pointed to a cluster of trees at the mouth of the forest. "They come out on this night especially. Go see, go see!"

Melody ran ahead, her yellow dress and flower garland disappearing into the black. "Get a torch, for goodness' sake! And don't go too deep. Just at the brink there." Pa put his big, dry hand on Layla's shoulder to stop her from running off.

"I know where Pa keeps his torch," Allie said, tearing off towards the house with her long dark hair sailing behind her like a cape. But Melody didn't wait for the others and she didn't come back to them that night. Layla asked Rowan to go and find Melody, but he wouldn't leave her side. Allie wouldn't help her look either, she was distracted, saying that she was sure she'd just seen little dots of lights circling the bluebells.

"Those must have been the faeries, like Mrs Hanigan said!" Layla saw nothing out there in the forest and went to bed feeling uneasy. That joy she saw in Mrs Hanigan's eyes was gone for good when Melody returned the next morning and said that some man in the forest had forced her to make a baby. Everyone's Pa and uncles and brothers marched into the forest that day but came back perplexed and anguished: neither the cottage nor the man could be found.

Layla's shoulder now aches and she must stop to take a moment's rest. She crouches down on her haunches, lets the axe slip from her aching palm and Rowan circles her, sniffing at the boots Pa gave her. They are slightly too big but he insists they will last a lifetime, and so Layla fills them with thick, knitted socks. Her small, flat feet throb in these boots now. Layla hears a rustle between her jagged breaths, but Rowan must have heard it some seconds before, as he is on his way towards a moss-caked log to inspect it. Layla stands up again and turns her head up to the sky, where the sun is pouring down its light. Layla takes it in her arms as if it will charge her with power. "He won't get me and he'll never get Allie." It was the evening before, the height of the harvest moon, when Allie thought she might find the faery folk again.

"I thought this night was special too," Allie had explained through tears, her forearm sore from where Ma had dragged her back to the house.

"You're not to go in there ever again! Is that understood?" Ma said in a tone they had never heard from her before, which escaped through her gritted teeth. Pa was resting deep in bed upstairs and no would tell him about Allie running across the meadow. Earlier that evening, Rowan had nipped at Layla's ankles to warn her of her sister's absence. It only took Layla seconds to realise that something was wrong. Layla and Ma burst through the door and sprinted across the meadow like two cheetahs. Layla lost her breath first. Ma found Allie at the start of the forest, where Layla finds herself now. Allie had whispered to Layla as they lay nose to nose in bed that night, that there was a man with a big smile who was coming towards her just before Ma arrived.

Layla strides on and Rowan bounds out from behind the log, abandoning his inspection of what is most likely squirrels rustling to join her, and deeper into the forest they go. "He won't get me with smiles. He won't get me with sweets. I'll take his head clean off before he can touch me." The further in they go, the thicker the smell of pine and moss becomes. She smells the various flowers and the earthiness of the trees, and on any other day, Layla would want to take this forest fragrance and bottle it. But today she is looking for the rot in the forest, the poison trying to choke anything that comes near it. "Where is he?" Layla says and looks down at Rowan, whose eyes squint in the sunlight, looking like two thin streaks of black ink.

Layla looks back to check which path they've taken and hopes that they can find their way out again. They walk on into the belly of the forest, where the sunlight is stolen away. The hairs on Layla's arm prickle. Rowan's fur moves a little in the breeze. The green around them grows dark, and up ahead Layla catches a wink of a red-coloured roof between branches. She has definitely been in this part of the forest before and this cottage was never here. Layla stops walking and so does Rowan. "That's his house there, Rowan. We're here." She switches the axe from her aching left hand to her still strong right and they each place one foot carefully in front of the other towards the front steps. A few birds chirp and the chimney puffs and Layla believes she can smell blueberries. The air feels thicker and warmer with the burning of a stove, which can be felt through the half-open window. A pale-blue curtain flutters and Layla draws her breath up heartily into her lungs. Rowan sniffs at the steps, his black triangular ears bobbing up and down. Sweat drops from Layla's forehead and into her eyes, stinging them for a moment. She can hear her own pulse, she can smell her own sweaty skin, but she moves her lips to chant again, silently, "He won't get me. He won't get me." But Rowan can hear her; his ear darts backwards and the tip of his nose twitches.

"Hello?" a voice calls invitingly from behind the orange-painted door. Layla raises the axe like she's seen Pa do; Rowan crouches low with his legs slightly spread. "Come in! Come in!" says the voice again and, at the turning of the handle and the creak of the door, Layla pushes through the aches in her arms, ready to swing, and thinks Pa's axe could be a hero.

The Animal Ball

THE INVITATION SAID, "Come one, come all," but what the hosts of the Barrington Masked Winter Ball meant on that sparkly piece of silver card was, in fact, "You've been chosen to attend because of your elegance and prestige." A beautiful, iridescent, paper snowflake sealed the carefully marked envelopes in which they were sent. Mrs Barrington had spared no cost for this event and she sought to dazzle her guests for one night during the gloomy, dark winter when all had been spent at Christmas, the New Year cheer was over, and people had resumed the dullness of their lives, which seemed to be exacerbated by this cold, bleak season. But for the ball on this night, angels must have heard the request for enchantment because the whitest snow twirled down in little wisps, making the Barrington residence look magical in the twilight. The invitation also specifically stated that all costumes were to be in the theme of animals, and so bears, foxes, birds and all sorts of other creatures glided up the stone path in their flamboyant and decadent gowns and masks towards the promise of drink, dance and other sociable delights, with the added pleasure of a concealed identity.

Mrs Barrington had decided to be a swan and her husband, a cardinal. She had made sure that his scarlet red, velvet suit fit just perfectly before she made the final touches to her own white, du chin satin dress, wings and mask. Mr Barrington gave her a kiss before he put on his feathered, scarlet cape and mask: a small red beak, attached to a blast of black feathers around his eyes, cheeks, chin and chest. Mrs Barrington was pleased with her swan wings, which could have just as easily passed for celestial wings. And that's how she felt as she swept white powder across her cheekbones: celestial, empowered and not of this world. And through the door to her own ballroom she entered, making her appearance a little later than her guests so that she could hear all at once the gasps and marvels and wonder as to who this beauty was.

Everything was frosted, as if kissed by the Snow Queen herself. Servers sauntered around in white fur and glittered faces, carrying glass platters of champagne glasses that were rimmed with sugar. The six dramatically large and arched windows that ran along the length of the ballroom had their usual heavy, velvet, red curtains replaced with long, white voile, and teardrop glass ornaments hung from the ceiling, winking light across the wooden floor as they gently twirled. There was a tower the size of a tent of macaroons, which were peppermint both in colour and flavour, and the ice sculpture centrepiece sat on a stage of its own and had everyone mesmerised by its craftsmanship. It was a scene from a fairy tale: a castle towered over two misfit lovers who were holding hands, frozen in their dance. And the most intriguing piece of all, which had all the guests wondering how it was carved so intricately, was the bell jar containing a single rose with its perfect petals, thorns and all. The fox tried to touch it and was quickly reprimanded by a server passing by.

There was a cellist and a violinist for entertainment, and,

for a bit of fun, a fortune teller dressed as a snow owl sat at her glittered glass table in the corner, reading people's cards. The badger scratched his head under his puffy black-and-white mask when the owl revealed to him that someone he loved was keeping secrets. The peacock was told that she'd soon come into good fortune and the lynx confirmed that there was in fact a baby on the way. As the champagne soaked its way through people's hearts, the queue for the fortune-telling snow owl grew longer. "I wonder if she'll mention my wedding," the raccoon said to the toad. "I wonder if she'll put my bad luck to an end," the boar said low under his breath. In her cloak of black-speckled white feathers and round, moon-like, fluffy mask, the fortune teller looked like a figure of the divine herself; the guardian of heaven's gates, telling all their fates and dooms: "To the underworld you will go for your indiscretions. You know what I speak of!" Some laughed if off to be hogwash, some tongues were silenced with fret. And although it was the swan that felt she held the power here, the snow owl seemed to be drawing all the guests into her spell.

The cardinal and the swan didn't dance together at all, but every now and again he'd seek her from across the room. While he was in deep conversation with the rainbow fish whose mask was made of a thousand sequins from iridescent to yellow, then orange then blue, her dress very much the same with a tail to match, the cardinal saw his swan gliding across the ballroom with purpose. She was looking about her, left and right, and then she disappeared through the door that led to the east wing of their home. The only thing in that wing was Mrs Barrington's studio, where she kept all her wooden sculptures. It was a hobby that turned into obsession some years ago when she discovered she could "trap spirits in wood." First it was a cat, then a dragon, then a gargoyle, and then a fairy. His wife would sweat over her piece of sugar maple, her fingers calloused and gripping tightly onto her gouge, jaw clenched in focus. It perplexed him as to how a woman who enjoyed the graces and luxuries of a privileged life so much would want to work like a common labourer for hours in solitude. She'd only ever shown her pieces of work to her husband, but she assured him that one day it would be revealed to the world. Maybe she'd still be alive when that happened, maybe not. But she believed she possessed some kind of genius and Mr Barrington, upon seeing what her self-taught skills produced, didn't ever dispute that. The cardinal thought to follow her and was trying to break off the rainbow fish's story about her young Dexter who would be starting his career as a cardiologist in the coming autumn, but was interrupted by a server who came to them with a tray of mini white cakes, decorated in edible glitter. "Vanilla frost cake, madam?" The rainbow fish lifted her sequined mask and shoved two cakes into her mouth and the cardinal took that as his cue to excuse himself. He dodged the antlers of the stag, who danced with the Persian cat, spitting out some of her grey mink that flew off from her stole and into his mouth as she swished. The hare was laughing heartily at the ferret's jokes, doubled over and clutching at his brown cashmere jumper; the cardinal moved him to one side and then bumped into a squirrel who he was sure was his niece, Eleanor. The auburn curls that peeked out from behind her brown velvet ears gave her away. She giggled and apologised for the collision and the cardinal would have stopped to speak with her, delighted to be in the company of family, but he was concerned about the swan and why she had left her ball.

Two hours into the party and the gentle melodies of the string musicians were swapped for the bouncier tunes of a piano. A wolf sat at the shiny, black grand, his grey and black tail hanging out of his tux and over the stool he was sitting on. His mask was made of felt, his furrowed brows of fluffy wool, and his snout was long and bulbous; it was a wonder that he could even see the keys over it. The dance floor thickened with more bodies. Limbs flailed and gowns spun. And in stepped a guest that the snow owl in particular was watching. She was taking a break from dealing cards and giving messages and was now stretching her legs by hovering around the white-chocolate fountain, sipping her champagne. A robin had come in from who knows where, but she smiled at his appearance. He was wearing a brown tweed suit, a white shirt and a stark red scarf. His brown mask had a petite beak, the eyeholes were very small and he wore an oversized brown skullcap, which covered his ears. His hands were covered in brown leather gloves; this guest really didn't want his identity to be given away. The robin weaved his way through the dance floor, his head very still and his body stiff. He stepped this way and that to avoid the field mouse and the butterfly, who were doing some sort of tango.

Outside, the snowflakes thickened and the sky looked like an enormous pillow fight had taken place; icy, misty feathers flew about in something slightly less than a blizzard. The cardinal had seen it when he made his way down the corridor of portraiture, some paintings collected by his grandparents, some by himself. He was heading in the direction of his swan's studio when he saw that to his right, the side entrance that led to the orchard, only ever used by Mrs Barrington, was open. The wooden door was trying its best to resist the push from the frosty air and the cardinal thought it strange that she would go out into such weather all by herself. As he approached the door, he thought he saw something on the white ground outside. Even though his small eyeholes gave him very little vision, there was definitely something there that shouldn't be. He bent down to pick up the ice rose that should have still been in the bell jar in the centrepiece of the ball. The petals had only melted slightly. One or two of the thorns had broken off, and where it had been snapped from the ice sculpture, the end of the stem was sharp and was coloured with blood. This had been a weapon and the user most certainly thought that it would vanish into the bed of snow before it was found. The cardinal's breath grew shallow, both from panic and from the winter air. He didn't think his wife could be capable of such things. Who would she have harmed? He needed to confront her before anybody else found out that someone had been hurt He pushed the ice rose into the earth with his shoe, giving it a proper burial, and went back into the wing in order to find the swan.

The door to the studio was locked and his wife had told him she would keep it locked during the party in case of nosy guests, but the cardinal had his own set of keys and quickly took out the bunch from his pocket and unlocked the door. The swan wasn't in there and everything seemed to look as it usually did when it wasn't in use: the workbench was clear, the tools were tidied away on the wall rack and the finished sculptures were in their places, all except one. His wife's latest masterpiece, the life-sized man that she had worked on for months and was so proud of, was missing. The cardinal remembered the day she had finished him. She had walked around him in circles, checking his proportions: his legs were that of a man, his torso was that of a man, his arms, neck and face – everything about him was perfect. He had a relaxed expression but a gaze fixed straight ahead. She'd carved his hair thick and neat and had given him boots, trousers, a shirt and a jacket. "Isn't he marvellous?" she'd said, beaming, and then tried a few names out loud for her sculpture for fun. "Do you think he looks like an Oscar, or a Paul or a Tristan?" Mr Barrington couldn't give her any names; he was stunned by what he saw: this wooden man was so lifelike.

But now he was gone and the cardinal couldn't fathom how. He needed to find his wife and speak to her about it. Just before he was about to close the studio door, something caught his eye on the floor. It was a black feather that must have fallen from someone's costume. He picked it up, twirled it with his fingers as if inspecting it like this would remind him of who could have been wearing such feathers. And then his eyes fell to the door of the cupboard where the swan kept her varnishes and lacquers; he felt compelled to open it. And when he did, a raven fell onto him. In horror, he threw the heavy body to the floor and jumped back. There was something dark and sticky seeping from the black-feathered cloak. The cardinal bent down to touch it; it was blood. He removed the big, Venetian-style beak and realised that he'd seen this man's face before, in a photo that his wife had tried to hide from him in the secret compartment of her jewellery box along with a letter that he had hoped he'd never have to mention. Surely this man had never been invited to the ball. This man was his wife's former lover from many years ago, and now he was dead.

"Dear owl, tell me my fortune," the robin said, now standing with her by the white-chocolate fountain. The bear was trying to lean across to dip a marshmallow in the fountain's flow but kept knocking over the ice-skater statue on the table with his large tummy. The snow owl stepped to one side to give him more room, linked her arm with the robin's, and led him to her table.

"Let's deal a card, shall we?" The robin sat down and adjusted his shirt and jacket. He could tell she was smiling behind her mask; he caught her blue eyes sparkling. She slowly took her deck of cards and spread them across the table; she paused, looked up at him and then chose one card from the middle and slid it towards herself. Before she could turn it over, the swan was by the robin's side, tapping on his shoulder.

"You're supposed to be gone," the swan whispered, her diamond drop earrings swinging as she spoke.

"Can't I enjoy the ball, just for a little while?" he teased.

"Oh, let him stay, swan. Everything's all done now; we can all relax," the snow owl said and then turned over the card and clapped her hands together with delight at what she saw. "Oh goodness, it's the tower!" Both the swan and robin looked at the picture on the card. It was of a building collapsing and there was fire burning through each window. "Something is going to come tumbling down."

⤳

A figure of scarlet red flounced through the ballroom towards her – her husband was coming right for her and she told herself to stay calm. What could he know? And then a white rabbit stopped him in his tracks. "Splendid garb! Are you a parrot? Oh no, you can't be, you've got no blue or yellow on you," the rabbit said, almost sloshing her drink straight out of her glass as she gestured. She was wearing a short-sleeved white dress made of alpaca and wore white silk gloves and white satin heels. Her blonde hair was braided around her head like a crown and her rabbit ears seemed to have been custom made to match her dress. Her white ceramic mask only covered her eyes and was rounded at the cheeks; her lips were painted a bright candyfloss pink.

"I'm a cardinal bird," the swan's husband replied, a little too curtly. He then excused himself in a more polite tone and continued to avoid the swirling dancers; a duck, an otter, a zebra and a goldfish were showing off their rather elegant performance of the waltz in pairs. "I wonder if I could speak with you a moment, dear," he said in her ear, trying not to give away his urgency. She followed him to the quiet, far corner of the ball and stood by the wall of candelabras and paintings reminiscent of Degas. "Could you please explain why there is a dead body in your studio?" The swan was good at faking surprise but not good enough to pass her own husband's in-terrogation. He saw her neck vein twitch a little.

"Pardon?" she asked, mocking shock.

"I want this tidied away as much as you do, so please explain it so we can get rid of it all properly." The swan kept up her charade, saying that she didn't know what he meant and then asked panicked questions about who could have got into her studio. Only her husband had a key and perhaps someone was trying to frame her. "Someone has been murdered and this someone was not invited to the party. I intend to find out who did it. I've got my eyes peeled for anyone looking suspicious," he told her, scanning her outfit for a speck of blood, sweat or any sign of a struggle, but she was spotless, fresh, and perfectly intact. She didn't do it herself, but she knew something all right.

"Who was it that was murdered?" she asked. The cardinal said he'd never seen the man before. She played with her diamond earrings and then said, "But, my dear, this is a masked ball. How on earth will we find the killer? Perhaps they've left already?" The cardinal muttered something about finding out from the snow owl and then headed back into the crowd. The swan looked over at the fortune teller's table and saw that the robin had vanished.

"Oh dear! The rose has gone!" the butterfly exclaimed, her glitter mask flickering between pink and purple with her movements. She pointed to the empty bell jar and the panther and the swan, who were within earshot, came over to look.

"Who would take that?" the panther asked and shook his black suede mask; one of his small round ears was slipping from his hair. The swan kept quiet.

"Shame. It was so beautiful. And someone else obviously thought so too," the toad interjected. He'd been gobbling some cake when he came over to marvel at the ice sculpture.

"Well they can't keep it for long. It'll melt," the panther

said before leaving them to find his deer friend. The swan looked about the ball and thought how wonderful everything still looked.

"Do you know what has happened here tonight?" the cardinal asked the snow owl. He had waited his turn in the queue behind the dove and the stag. The dove was told to end her unhappy marriage and the stag was warned to be careful with his money. The wolf at the piano was slowing down the music now; the tunes were becoming soft and romantic. It was a good thing too, the cardinal thought, this ball would soon be over.

"Plenty has happened here tonight!" the snow owl cheered, the feathers on her broad shoulders swayed a little as she moved.

"You know what I mean," he replied, his body suddenly growing very hot in his velvet suit. He asked her who had been wearing the raven costume.

"I think you know," she said slowly and shuffled her cards in her pale, milky hands.

"So do you, evidently," he replied, looking across the room again quickly for the whereabouts of the swan or for anyone who was behaving oddly. The swan was now dancing with the boar. How could she still be enjoying herself so? "Tell me everything, and whatever she's paying you for this evening, I'll triple it," he said low and clear.

"Would you like to hear a story, mister cardinal bird, sir?"

"There once was a raven and a swan, and a long time ago, they fell in love. Now the raven had his own burdens to bear, for he was committed to someone else, let's call her the rat, shall we? She was a pest for the raven and the swan; they couldn't fully be together while she was around. The swan wanted the raven all to herself, but the raven was weak and couldn't leave the rat, but begged the swan to stay and love him until he could find his courage to end the situation. The rat grew suspicious and began searching through the raven's belongings to find clues of an affair. She rifled through his wardrobe, checked the pockets of his clothes, and then found a napkin, tucked in between a book of poetry – how ironic – and this napkin was imprinted with a lipstick mark. The rat never wore such a shade of red but had seen that very colour on someone's lips before. She had met the swan at a dinner party that the raven had accompanied her to just before his actions became peculiar and his affections towards her cooled. The rat sniffed out the swan and visited her at her home. The swan offered her a drink before the rat could vocalise her accusations. The rat drank down her drink to calm her nerves, and thus the rat was poisoned. The raven promised that he wouldn't utter a word about what the swan had done for them to be together and the official report goes that the rat had ended her own life. The body had been carefully moved back to her own home. It wasn't long before the swan grew bored of this hassle of a relationship; the raven became more needy and his love for her was suffocating. She left him shortly after that and he tried to look for her but she was long gone. A year or two later, the swan met a cardinal. Now, I think you know what happens there. And the swan found a way to calm her guilty conscience by taking up a hobby. The swan to this day, carves figures from wood and her greatest treasure is a life-size and very real looking man. Let's go back just a touch. The raven had managed to find the swan and sent her a letter of warning: he would expose what she had done to his lover and ruin her. She fretted a little but didn't panic too much and decided to call upon a snow owl she knows – who will be paid handsomely for this, might I add, and who has magical powers beyond your wildest dreams. The swan asked her to cast a very unique and glorious spell. The swan sent a letter to the raven, which included politely that she'd like to talk with him and that perhaps she had made a mistake in leaving him. She said she'd missed him and would he come to her winter masked ball. It would be perfect for their discretion. She'd wear all white and he must wear all black and acknowledge her when he arrived. Here's the part that's really interesting: the swan hasn't missed him at all. In fact, she's been wanting to get rid of him and get rid of everything he knows. So the spell the snow owl can cast is very special, as I say. It can make inanimate objects animate. Perfect for a wooden man to turn into human for a night – or rather a robin – dispose of the raven, and then be back in his wooden, lifeless form again before anyone could know. And if anyone did happen to catch the robin in the act, who would believe them when they told the authorities that the killer was the sculpture?"

It was just past one in the morning when a few guests started to leave the ball and stagger their way out into the cold, snowy night to wait for their drivers, who would have some difficulty coming and going in this weather. The bear was holding onto the Persian cat, whose legs couldn't find their coordination. Her mink stole was slipping off her shoulders, and her grey cat mask was cocked to one side. The panther was waiting for the deer to say her goodbyes and join him by the front door; the rainbow fish was finishing off the last of the cakes on the table, as she hated to think that they'd go to waste. The goldfish and the zebra were still swaying on the dance floor; the sleepy song the wolf was playing was causing them to doze off on each other's shoulders. The squirrel didn't want her conversation to end with the charming badger, who felt compelled to talk about his reading with the fortune-teller, both of them sat on silver chairs facing one another in deep discussion. And even though the guests were fading, the sparkles and glitter of the ballroom were not; the ice sculpture to everyone's surprise showed no signs of melting. It was still solid and beautiful, but all agreed that it was nevertheless a great shame that the rose had been stolen. The snow owl began packing up her cards into her wooden box, ready to see the night end. The swan went over to the wolf and told him that this song was to be the last and the cardinal started thanking the guests and informed them that the ball was coming to an end. "We've had a lovely evening, Mr Barrington, thank you," most of them said, now knowing who he was. The cardinal disappeared before the wolf received his payment from the lady of the house and went on his way. The swan went over to the snow owl to explain that she'd have her payment the next day as she didn't have any more cash on her.

"Oh no, all that has been sorted with your husband," the snow owl replied, stroking the feathers of her cloak.

"What do you mean?" The swan gulped down the lump in her throat, discreetly she thought, but the snow owl saw it.

"I think you ought to talk to him about it."

She found him waiting in her studio, standing by the window with his mask gone, his scarlet suit looking more like burgundy in the gloomy light. "They all had a wonderful time, didn't they, darling?" he said to her. She removed her mask and went to take off her wings also, but then she thought that they'd give her strength in this situation somehow so kept them on.

"Yes, they did." She stepped a little closer and looked at her wooden man, who was back in his place where he should be. Her husband met her glance for a moment and then turned back to the window and giggled at the Persian cat drunkenly playing with the snow. Some jokes and cackles came from those still waiting for their cars to arrive. The snow was easing up now. It would settle; all would be calm soon.

"The snow owl said you've taken care of her payment." The swan didn't know the tone with which she should be speaking and so it was coming out a little strangled.

"Yes, I've written her a cheque and have given her a very attractive sum for the revelations she's given me this evening." The cardinal walked towards his swan, looked at her face for a moment and tried to remember when it was pure. Had it ever been? Did he just think he had seen it before? He watched her eyes flicker over to the cupboard where the raven was, probably wondering if her husband had disposed of it for her. The cardinal brushed one of her wings with his shoulder as he walked past and headed for the door behind her. She turned to face him.

"I'm just going to let you sit in here for a while and think about what it is your witch friend may have told me. Night

night, dear." The cardinal struck a match from the box he'd pulled out of his pocket and threw it at the wooden man that was stood next to his wife; it instantly caught fire. The swan screamed at the sight of her masterpiece disintegrating in the flames. "Oh, and I spilled some lacquer all over your studio by accident earlier on. Sorry about that." And with those last words to his wife, he left the room, shut the studio door and locked it. He walked away, hearing her scream and bang her fists on the inside of the door.

Together, the snow owl and the cardinal watched the Barrington residence get eaten by the fire room by room, a bright orange glow making its way down the halls, to the central staircase, across the ballroom where they had all just been dancing the night away, and then to the kitchen. And up it would go until the whole building collapsed. The last of the guests' cars had pulled out of the drive before anyone noticed the smoke. "What will you do, Mr Barrington?" The snow owl asked him, now dressed in a white fur, much like the ones the servers had been wearing.

"A fresh start, I think. I'm rather happy to let it all go. It's all been tainted with secrets and murder." The cardinal slipped into a reverie for a moment, of days passed that he had thought to be true happiness but had actually been lies. A loud noise broke him out of it then – something popped from the upstairs window, third from the right, sending balls of fire flying into the cold air. The snow owl's eyes widened at the display. "You'd better go home and get warm," the cardinal said, looking up at the indigo sky, his eyes squinting from the snowflakes falling. "The snow is starting up again."

The Cemetery Pilgrimage

LET'S OBSERVE A man. This man is walking hastily through the streets of Paris on All Hallow's Eve. He is heading for Père Lachaise, a cemetery famous for its star collection of bodies, of virtuosos and geniuses – painters, composers, writers and poets. Some died tragically, some died righteously, and this man is going to steal the essence of their talents. He will absorb them into himself through an ancient ritual he was given by a stranger. This ritual must be performed at the geniuses' graves. But he won't finish there at Père Lachaise: before sunrise on the first day of November, he must have completed this magic in the Pantheon, Giverny Church Cemetery, and Auvers-sur-Oise, where the rest of the desired corpses are buried. His targets are Frédéric Chopin, Marcel Proust, Oscar Wilde, Victor Hugo, Alexandre Dumas, Claude Monet and Vincent van Gogh. From them he will take their talent, their fame, their fruitfulness, their innovative thinking and their historical immortality.

But what would lead a man to such pursuits?

Let's watch him here. He is dressed in a slate-grey Hermes suit and is wearing mahogany-coloured brogues on his feet. Over this suit he wears a three-quarter-length tweed town coat in an even moodier grey, which he wears open to show off this favourite suit and his navy blue Armani scarf. This outfit makes him feel important; it tells people he has money and that he is stylish and smart, but this isn't entirely true. He once had money, not lots but some, but he lost it all. These items are actually hand-me-downs from an old colleague who can afford to give away a year-old Hermes suit and an Armani scarf for free. But this man here, whom we watch dodging Halloween partygoers and other pedestrians in the street, turning corners flustered and charged, has no job to wear these clothes to. He can only just about hang on to the apartment he's been renting in Montmartre since his second divorce. And as long as he is wearing his armour, he won't have to watch faces pity the crumbling man that is underneath it.

He makes a left off the main road, passing three women in costumes: a zombie in a short skirt, a witch and Marilyn Monroe. Marilyn is fortunate enough to have natural blonde hair, which she has curled and styled to perfection. Her white satin dress billows authentically in the autumn breeze. The witch has made less effort with her clothing, wearing a long black wig and, on top of that, a pointy hat made flimsily out of black card. She is carrying a broom that this man presumes she has bought in a homeware shop. Her face doesn't sport the usual ugly crooked nose and warts, but she has rather gone to great efforts to do her make-up beautifully. She wears a rich cherry-red lipstick and has sculpted her black eyebrows in the fashion of Elizabeth Taylor. The zombie has slashes across her cleavage, which she is clearly happy for eyes to be drawn to. Her brown hair has been teased and backcombed, and some fake blood has been strategically placed along the parting of her hair to make as if she has a gash on her head. Cuts and scrapes decorate her skin, large black circles have been painted under her eyes, her body has been painted a bluish-grey. He cannot tell if they are on their way to a party or on their way out of one; it is only 10 p.m. They are tipsy and wobble in their heels, arms draped over one another, silly smiles glowing white under all that make-up and face paint. He remembers his first wife, Francesca, never having to wear make-up at all. Her skin looked new every morning on the pillow next to him, her left dimple accenting her sleepy smile. He had focused on that dimple during the days she looked sick, when the cancer started to show itself. That dimple – that little mark of youth and happiness – couldn't be taken away.

This man is called Clyde Abrahams, and Clyde remembers being scared of Halloween night when he was a small boy, growing up in a small town in England. His father told Clyde and his younger sister, Laura, Gothic tales by candlelight. The kids on his street set out to frighten one another with elaborate and cruel pranks. Shrill screams could be heard outside. Clyde was afraid to peek out through the curtains and he was terrified to look under his bed, fearing he'd find evil ghosts that might drag him to hell, or werewolves that could shred his skin and gnaw their way into his guts while he was still alive. Laura would climb up to him from the lower bunkbed and together they'd sing happy songs to stop themselves from feeling frightened.

There is a brief moment here, where he thinks about Laura, who will never speak to him again. Some years ago there was an incident with Laura's husband, Mick. Mick trusted Clyde to help him set up a hotel business in Thailand. Clyde insisted on hiring the workmen. The workers disappeared with the money for the tools and parts and never returned. Mick had no choice but to wave his money goodbye and abandon the unfinished building. Clyde now thinks he should have been more apologetic at the time and attempted to put things right with Mick and his sister, but Clyde was drinking a lot back then. The memories are a blur: was he frogmarched out of the building when he lost his job, or did he leave by himself? Did anyone say goodbye? Was there a week when he didn't eat? Was that the time he found Francesca's broken watch under the sofa and cried until his lungs burned?

Tonight, Clyde can proudly say that he is feeling stronger. More than that – he is even brave enough to face the dark and unknown. He has, in fact, welcomed the other world into his life. He is exploring the supernatural. Since that day when he went as far as tying a piece of towing rope to the light fixture on the ceiling and putting it around his neck, then deciding he wasn't yet ready, he has felt a kinship with the spirit world. He had felt death enter the room then exit again, like a student walking into the wrong class. Clyde realised that there were mysterious and powerful things in existence; things that had tried to entice him to the other side before. And especially on this night in Paris, he is leaving his reality. Clyde is being accompanied by a ghost. This ghost will help him carry out his task of stealing the success he has always been so desperate for, from those who are no longer alive.

No one else can see a soldier with one hollow eye socket walking alongside Clyde down Rue du Chemin Vert, which will take them to their first cemetery. This soldier once answered to the name of Byrd and never by his first name of Dennis. He died on this land and not on the one he called home, and he does not look any more with his eyes but with his soul. They had started out together near the Bastille, away from the bar in which Clyde had been drinking with an old man he'd just met. After some hours of conversation, when they were to part ways, the old man told Clyde that Byrd would be waiting for him outside to begin their journey.

It had been a fairly normal night to begin with. Normal for Clyde meant eating a dinner of salad, green beans, a small piece of buttered bread and some grilled chicken on his one and only plate. He ate this dinner at the wobbly round table kept next to the window of his loft apartment. Through this window, there is a view of the far left curve of Sacré-Coeur, which sits between two ugly buildings. There are no Parisian balconies laced with flowerboxes, grand arched doors or clean white paint in his neighbourhood. He lives among those who struggle to sell their art and wish to shine like a brand new coin in a city already full of treasures. Clyde is also one of these people. He has struggled to find his way to not only make money, but to achieve recognition. No matter how hard he's tried, he has never managed to sustain admiration from anyone, not even his second wife. Only Francesca had ever been the one to look at him with light in her eyes. But that light had been extinguished. He would very, very much like for someone to see the sparkle in him – polish him up and put him somewhere special. And this was very much the subject of his conversation with the old man in the bar.

After dinner, Clyde continued with his usual routine of going for a walk to digest his meal. Watching the narrow, broken streets turn into wide boulevards and seeing the buildings grow wider and more opulent. Strolling as the neon signs and cluttered sidewalks give way to lampposts and ornate arches and turrets. He especially enjoys spotting a grotesque sitting on a roof looking down at him. It is the Gothic, the romantic and the hidden details that excite Clyde the most about this city. On this Halloween night, he took his usual route, feeling gratitude for the cool weather, which he prefers to the thick heat of the summer. He relaxed once the smells of his neighbourhood dissipated, smells that all together give off an aroma of a muddy newspaper dropped into a pile of rotten eggs. When he crossed over into more favourable areas, he breathed in the air and it reminded him of geranium and whipped cream. He wanted to reward himself with a drink - which he usually does more often than not on these walks - but Clyde never drinks in the same bar. He is, of course, not from this city, and it shows, having come to Paris only five months ago to start anew; he is always startled when someone speaks to him.

He didn't catch the name of the bar he walked into, but he liked the look of it being half empty. There was no music playing to intrude on his thoughts and no shiny young people to make him feel silly. The bar smelt of peanuts, soil and dried whisky. Alcohol had never been cleaned out of the carpet, he presumed. Clyde crossed one leg over the other, a habit he had whenever he wore a suit. He pulled out a notebook the size of a shop receipt and a miniature pencil he always carried from the inside pocket of his town coat.

This notebook contains a list, a list meant for his eyes only. In this list, Clyde writes down his failures. These date back to three years ago. He has two pages left in this notebook. The used pages threaten to come away from the binding; they have weakened and been worn from frequent use. Clyde reads these failures every day, over and over again, and usually before he goes to sleep. He wished to add to this list that today he failed to come up with a new business plan. Yesterday he failed to charm the bosses of an English bank; a month ago he failed to start a novel; a year ago he failed to be the man his second wife wanted him to be; three years ago he failed to receive a promotion and instead was fired and lost everything. And in between all this, he failed at making new friends, failed to impress those he admired, failed to paint, to learn an instrument, to study psychology, failed at being loved forever, and failed at making every day a successful one. The old man at the table to his left leaned over and asked in French what he was writing. Clyde simply replied, "Anglais," and the old man switched to perfect English. It was the first time Clyde had ever discussed his list with anyone.

And now, Clyde and Byrd arrive at Père Lachaise. The cemetery is guarded by high stone walls that are impossible to climb. Clyde inspects the doors, which are of course, bolted shut. "I thought it'd be gates, not doors," Clyde says to Byrd, now comfortable with speaking, as there is no one around who might think he is talking to himself.

"Well, that's what I'm here for," Byrd replies, and disappears into the door the way an ice cube might melt rapidly in a glass of warm water. Clyde looks around him: there are a few pedestrians in the distance, but none who can see him standing here in the shadows. He hears a lock break from the inside and the large heavy door creaks open, just enough for him to slip through.

"You want to be famous, is that it?" the old man had asked Clyde earlier, as the two of them started on their second drinks. The bar was filling up and the chatter around them covered up the confidential details of their conversation from unwanted ears.

"Doesn't everybody?" Clyde replied.

No, this isn't true, thought the old man; not everybody wants to be famous, but everyone wishes to be successful.

"I do want something. I want to be talented and admired. I want to be sought after." It felt good to say it out loud. If there is anything Clyde does have, it is pride. But this conversation didn't make him feel ashamed. After all, he believed he was just as entitled to success and happiness as everyone else. But what does often bruise Clyde's ego is feeling powerless. The old man told Clyde what Clyde had told himself many times before: that people have been coming to Paris for decades to find greatness – artists, musicians, writers. Clyde knew this already. He also knew that this romantic age of the greats was over and had been for a long time. Paris is just like any other city now, like London, like New York – it is hard to be special. But having someone else say it to him and quash his dreams was difficult to accept.

Clyde was willing to finish up his drink and head back to

his apartment at this point; talking about all this was only making him feel angry. But then the old man put his shaky hand on Clyde's sleeve and said, "Do you believe in the impossible, Mr Abrahams? If you do, I can help you."

"Proust first – he's the nearest," Byrd tells Clyde. "I know this cemetery like the back of my cold, dead hand." Even in the darkness, the cemetery feels vast and, ironically, like it is alive, like a large beast, a sleeping dragon even, that Clyde had just come upon. Byrd puts his hands together and a beam of light streams from his palms, lighting up the path ahead.

"You have powers," Clyde says, impressed.

"The dead have many powers, that's why you're here, isn't it?" Byrd replies. Clyde cannot look directly into Byrd's eye socket but looks at the rest of his face and body instead. He is an average-looking young man, like any wholesome English boy Clyde could have encountered in school, wanting to do his family proud when he grew up. The cemetery is plentiful, with graves, with trees, with nature. He imagines himself to be walking through an ordinary park as his feet creep along the grass.

"Did it hurt?" Clyde asks the soldier, who has stopped just a couple of paces ahead of him in front of the grave of Marcel Proust. Byrd knows he is referring to the wound that killed him.

"It didn't have time to hurt. If you're shot in the eye, you don't really have a moment to think about it. Your brain is instantly terminated. Everything is just gone."

❧

"There's an ancient ritual," the old man had said, speaking low across the table but clear enough for Clyde to hear him. "If this ritual is performed on the night of Halloween, where the veil between this world and the other is thin, one can summon the essence of those passed and absorb all the talents and abilities they had when they were alive." Clyde scoffed and took another sip of his wine, thinking that this old man was playing with him. But up until then, over the course of the evening, Clyde had grown fond of the old man, had even begun to trust him and respect his wisdom. "Take this," the old man had said, pulling out a tattered piece of paper from the pocket of his worn and fraying black blazer. The piece of paper seemed to have been torn from a book and showed the age of something that belonged in a museum. Clyde stared at the page. The writing was in a language he couldn't understand and wasn't even sure was spoken anymore. Was it Sanskrit? Ancient Hebrew? Clyde looked up into the old man's dark brown eyes, which seemed to carry the weight of a very long and complicated life. Clyde gave him a blank expression, pressing him to explain what was written. The old man took one hand and waved it gently over the page in Clyde's hands as if he were checking the warmth coming off a radiator. When he took his hand away, the writing was in English.

"How did you?" Clyde was shocked, but laughed in amazement, his eyes wide with hunger for more of the magic he had just witnessed.

"You believe in the impossible, don't you?" The old man smiled.

"Why Proust?" Byrd asks Clyde now.

"The man wrote a three-thousand-page novel, he was a thinker, and I want that sort of stamina, that vastness of thought." Clyde takes the dagger that was given to him by the old man, which he has been carrying around nervously in the pocket of his suit trousers. He pricks his finger with it until a bead of crimson forms at the surface of his skin. He tilts his finger and holds it over the ground by the grave and allows drops of his blood to fall onto the earth. He begins to chant the summoning spell he was given.

"This spell is believed to have been given to a sorcerer directly by a god. Many Egyptian kings have used it, witches and druids, too. Only a few have lived to pass it on," the old man had explained.

"Why didn't they live to pass it on?" Clyde had asked, nicely warmed by the second glass of wine he had just finished.

"Because this is not a gift, dear boy, this is a contract. When you perform this ritual, you are agreeing that you only get your incredible success for five years. Then you die." When Clyde had asked how one was supposed to enjoy his riches for just five years, the old man replied, "It isn't the riches that matter. You want greatness, don't you? Well, fame is immortality, it will live forever beyond you. Five years is plenty of time to enjoy money, if that's what you want. But what has your life been so far?" The old man took the piece of paper back from Clyde's hands and gave him a long hard look. "So, do you want this or not?"

Several voices flood into Clyde's ears in whispers all at once but he cannot decipher what is being said. He sees a swirl of smoke, or perhaps that is a soul, Marcel Proust's soul, appearing before the grave. Clyde feels a vibration, like a surge of electricity buzzing in his feet; it works its way up his legs and hits him in the gut, then spreads to his arms, his back, up his neck and into his head. His spine, his fingers and even his brain are tingling. The swirl of smoke turns into little specks of light, like silver glitter floating through the air. The tendril begins to take shape; it twists into the form of a cord, a wire or a piece of rope. It hovers in front of Clyde at brow level. On the other end of the cord, a silver-flecked figure forms in the shape of a man. The cord connects to the head of this figure and the loose end in front of Clyde attaches itself to the centre of his forehead. "The cord will pass the genius from him to you. Just allow it to pour in," Byrd assures Clyde. A bright light gushes into Clyde's mind; it feels like a sharp rapid wind rushing through a tunnel. It is cold and it heightens the vibrations he feels through the whole of his body. When all the genius has been drawn in, the cord breaks away and disappears into the figure, which turns from silver sparkles to a black silhouette and then is gone.

Clyde lets out a hearty laugh. "Yes, I feel it! I can feel it!" He clenches his fists as if to contain the euphoria within him. The whispers cease and the cemetery quietens again. "Come on, Byrd, we have plenty more to do. Who's next?" Byrd sets off up the main path and Clyde follows swiftly, but looks back twice at the grave that appears just as still and lifeless as it did when they first arrived.

"Chopin next," Byrd says over his shoulder. "Watch your step – the cemetery gets wilder the deeper we go."

Frédéric Chopin is buried under a grave of cream-coloured stone and is guarded by a stone woman, who bows romantically over the piano virtuoso, with her gown in ripples across her body and gathered over her legs. Clyde bows in response, out of reflex and out of excitement. He performs the ritual in the same way: he gives his blood to the grave, but this time the droplets stain the stone below, as there is no earth there to drink it. He summons the soul of Chopin and the swirl of smoke turns into a silver glitter cord again and connects Clyde to the soul of the pianist. Clyde receives the sounds of the composer's nocturnes, the beautiful, sensitive tones of his piano pieces, falling into his ears like raindrops. Clyde grins and closes his eyes, entranced by the music. He breathes in deeply as the genius of the composer rushes into his hungry mind. When it has all been funnelled in, the sparkles vanish and the grave darkens again. This feeling is definitely worth living on for, Clyde thinks. "Byrd, do you know I'm half tempted to run off and find a piano. I have ideas! I can still hear music, except it's not Chopin's anymore, it is my own!" Clyde runs his hands through his wavy, black hair. The tingles are back in his fingers; they again run up and down his spine.

"We most certainly can do that, or we can carry on with completing the pilgrimage," Byrd replies, putting his hands into pockets.

"I want to carry on," Clyde says, now full of energy and zest.

"Well then, follow me. Oscar Wilde awaits."

Clyde walks carefully up the steps that bring the cemetery

to its next level, where it takes on its notorious labyrinthine form. Clyde feels the stirrings of the cemetery grow stronger; perhaps he can sense squirrels running across the lawn towards trees or perhaps he is feeling the dead waking up – he cannot tell. Either way, there are creatures present and they are watching him. "I shall go home and write a novel when we're finished tonight." Clyde rubs his hands together and admires Wilde's eccentric grave, thinking that only a man like him would have such an absurd tomb as this: an Egyptian sculpture resting on top an oblong mount, so odd and out of place. "Did you ever do anything like that, Byrd? Did you ever write or play music?"

The soldier looks away from Clyde and into the blackness around them. "I didn't have a chance to find out what it was I loved to do. I was in the war when I could barely call myself an adult. As a boy, I concentrated on school. I was raised to just be a good boy – that was all – just be a good boy," Byrd finally replies.

"You served your country. You were brave," Clyde tells him.

"I don't think a soldier would ever use the word 'brave', sir."

Byrd wishes to know why Clyde needs to do this, why his life isn't complete without this outrageous success, but he doesn't ask him. He pities Clyde, but pities himself more because in his own short life, he had never tried to put himself first.

It is past midnight when Clyde and Byrd leave Père Lachaise. They must make their way across the city from the east back into the centre, towards the Pantheon, where Clyde is excited to take the talents of Victor Hugo and Alexandre Dumas. "Such great books, Byrd. Did you ever read them?" Clyde says when they take a turn down a quiet road, which parallels the main route to the Seine.

"I don't know which books you're referring to." The soldier ghost walks just as a live soldier would, arms stiff and straight, swinging in time with the rhythm of his steps; he looks ahead and never to his feet.

"Oh, come on. *Les Misérables? The Count of Monte Cristo?*"

Byrd nods with recognition. "Great works," Byrd says in a thin voice.

They cross the bridge by Notre Dame; Clyde looks up at the stained glass windows of the cathedral and sighs with wonderment. It is only minutes before they reach the Pantheon with its Greek columns and majestic dome that sits on top of the building like a king on his throne. "This is why I came to Paris, Byrd. The beauty of it hasn't faded in centuries. Sure, you have the bars, the clubs, this cosmopolitan scene, but I can feel all the great things that have happened here." Clyde is reminded now of when he first arrived five months ago. It wasn't necessarily because of Paris's beauty that he came here; it was rather because he was desperate to run away and hide from England.

"Ever married?" Byrd asks Clyde, as they stand discreetly at the foot of the steps of the Pantheon.

Clyde looks sideways at the entrance, waiting for pedestrians to clear away. "Twice," he says quietly.

"And?" Byrd prompts him for more.

"The last was divorce, the first I became a widower." With the memory of Francesca's death coming to mind again, Clyde is no longer standing in the streets of Paris in the middle of a breezy autumn night. He is in Sussex on a fresh spring morning, watching a coffin being lowered into the ground, his own weeping drowned out by Francesca's mother crying out to God. Byrd does not push for any more information, but stands with Clyde in silence for a few minutes and wonders how Clyde would feel if someone were to visit his wife's grave and steal the essence of her. And almost as if Clyde is thinking the same thing, he shakes his head as if not to explore such thoughts. "Are we ready?" Clyde says to Byrd, and straightens the lapels on his town coat. He leaves their sad conversation where it hangs, by the steps, and walks up to the entrance of the Pantheon.

"We'll have to make this one quick," Byrd says to him. "You have more of a chance of getting caught."

And so this man and his ghost companion charge on through the night. Clyde is bursting with inspiration and feels his newly-acquired talents swimming through his body, as if all it would take is to put a pen in his hand and the gifts would flow from him and onto blank pages and music sheets. He knows the spell is working. He knows that life will never be the same again. More importantly, he is beginning to understand what it actually feels like to be alive.

It is four in the morning when they are at their last grave in Giverny. To save time, Clyde had taken a taxi there, first stopping at Auvers-sur-Oise to collect the essence of Vincent van Gogh and then down to the old property of Claude Monet, the cab driver unawares that the ghost of a World War II soldier was along for the ride. Clyde had done his best to not speak to Byrd as they sat in the back seat together, but looked at him occasionally to check he was still there. Clyde was sitting on Byrd's good side; he could finally admire the handsomeness of Byrd's blue eye and his smooth, youthful skin.

The genius of Monet dances its way into Clyde so delicately that he does not feel cold like those from Père Lachaise and the other graves. It is warm and blends wonderfully with all the others that circulate in him. Peace descends upon him with this final spell; there is relief that he is a different man, an able man. "Oh, it's just beautiful." Clyde is marvelling at the famous lily pond as they stand on Monet's little red bridge. The sky is turning from indigo to powder blue, which sends a little more light to the weeping willows, the water and the luscious orange hues of autumn. Byrd sends his beam of light across the pond to highlight its serene tones. Soon everything will turn golden in the light of the rising sun. "I'm seeing what Monet could see. I'm looking at the sky with van Gogh's eyes," Clyde says excitedly. "Ha! I have the vision of a painter, at last!" Clyde's senses are heightened; he draws in the blend of aromas around him: the algae of the pond, the crispness of morning dew, the sweetness of the grass and the charred scent of fallen leaves. He will paint this blend, he thinks to himself. He'll remember these smells and put colour to them on canvas.

Just as light breaks, someone comes to join them on the bridge. It is the old man from the bar. Clyde is surprised to see him and Byrd seems disappointed. It is time for him to go back to the other world. "Well done," the old man says to Clyde. "You did it. How do you feel?"

Clyde spreads his arms wide and tells him he feels wonderful.

"Enjoy your fame, Mr Abrahams," the old man says. "And I will see you in five years' time." The old man beckons for Byrd to stand beside him, as they will leave together.

"Why will you and I see each other in five years' time?" Clyde asks. The birds around them wake up, chirping emphatically overhead.

"Haven't you realised, Clyde? I'm a keeper of souls. This body may be eighty years old, but I am not this old man. My soul is older than you can comprehend. And yours is as fresh as a fawn. But it belongs to me now and I'll be waiting for you." And just as quickly as the old man appeared, he is gone again, taking Byrd with him. Clyde is left standing alone.

Clyde will meet his soldier companion again one day, but first he will start painting stunning and complex pieces of art. He will compose music to go with these pieces and showcase them at prestigious galleries. They will be bought for millions and his concertos tickets will sell out in hours. He will tour the world, exhibiting his work in national galleries everywhere; he will give a smug smile as his work is hung in London and he will enjoy visiting New York, Italy and Moscow, where the people adore him the most. He'll make good friends and great wealth and in his fourth year he will complete the novels, plays and essays he has been piecing together since he left Giverny on that November morning. He will die a legend on a summer's night in Paris, where he lives in his resplendent town house in Saint-Germain-des-Prés, in the comfort of his own bed. His death will be announced in newspapers worldwide, his fans will mourn him and he will be buried in Père Lachaise, where his success began.

And when the soul keeper comes for him, he will be pleased to go, because nothing was ever as meaningful as the Halloween night in Paris when he made a true friend. He will be happy to go to the other side, knowing that one day he may be the ghost companion for someone just like him. Clyde will save someone from giving up on life as well. He will encourage them to pursue their dreams.

He will go and find his soldier friend, who also once asked for a gift during the time he was alive. Byrd had prayed to the skies to make him a hero whilst on that boat to France. And his prayers were answered one wet and blustery day in Normandy, when he saved his sergeant from attack, and took a bullet in the eye. In his own way, Dennis Byrd will also never be forgotten by the world.

The Bouquet Witch

IT'S THE COLOURS that strike me most about flowers, how a bunch can pierce through a bleak room like a star-burst galaxy or sunlight pouring into a murky pond. It's as if nature is sitting in a vase in your room and is delivering to you a message of hope. It reminds you of better times past or makes you think of better times to come. It is nature's art, its expression of vitality, beauty and love – one usually begets the other. When one is struck by beauty, love trickles into the heart and the blood is pumped with an essence of vitality and euphoria. And after I visually feast on the flowers' colours, I touch them just before I smell them: the silkiness of their petals melts me; it is a kind touch on the skin, a gentle kiss. Then when I breathe in their scent, my mind is sucked into a dreamland. Some aromas can take me to a specific place or time. I do love a good rose. Who doesn't? My heart swells at the sight of a peony and I am delighted by Japanese cherry blossoms. And all of this beauty is in one single talisman, a keepsake from nature, and it is reassuring that nothing about it can disappoint you. Nothing about it will fool you, and that's why it was the perfect way for me to avenge the broken-hearted.

I met a witch who can cast darks spells on a bouquet of flowers. It delights their receiver just for a few moments before it kills them. I freed this witch from her water graveyard of a stone fountain; her soul had been trapped there for a hundred years.

But before I begin to tell you about Anastasia, let me go back to when I was a young girl. I had a next-door neighbour by the name of Mrs Edwin. I would often visit her for tea and we would sit in her tiny living room and she would tell me stories. She would tell me about her best friend, Annie, with whom she shared a little apartment in the city when she was young. Mrs Edwin – although, in these stories, she would refer to herself as Bette – suffered from a case or two of the blues when she was young, she'd told me. "It was because of love, always love," she'd said as she shook her head while smiling as if to make light of something that had gnawed at her for years. "Lack of love, too much love. Deep love with a man, thin love from my mother." Mrs Edwin told me that Annie used to cheer her up on a particularly low day by blowing up balloons and filling up their entire apartment with them. "She knew how to make me giggle." She wiped away a tear then as she spoke, perhaps shed from a delightful memory, perhaps because this one led onto a more painful one. I used to think that I'd quite like to meet Annie, or have a best friend of my own just like her. I would try to recreate Annie's jibes with my sister, Rosemary, but she wouldn't laugh. Her heart didn't tickle easily; it was a firm heart, and a serious one, and that kind of heart couldn't be softened without great effort. Mine was soft and open and it tried its best to ignore how lonely it was. It was always hopeful.

It was a small town where we lived, and it was difficult for me to find other children to play with, especially at school where I was a ghost to all, even though every single child was known by their first or second name and who their parents were. And outside of school when I did happen to meet a group of them congregating on the street in town or running together through the meadow, which I considered my territory, I always got the impression that something alienated me. I would speak and not be heard. I didn't look odd, I didn't dress strangely and I had a lot to say, but even my older sister didn't find me interesting. But at the age of twelve, when friendships truly began to matter, I was ostracised for no reason. Maybe it was just destiny for me to never have friends. So I made Mrs Edwin, the seventy-eight-year-old woman next door, my one and only confidante.

Aside from envying Mrs Edwin's great friendship with Annie, I also wished to encounter the kind of love that Mrs Edwin spoke of. Even the kind that perhaps happened during the tougher days when men and boys would be dancing with you one minute, then gone the next. And if they ever returned, they may be damaged, or worse, carried in a wooden box decorated with a flag and flowers. Flowers still, even in times of death and bereavement, promise you that life is beautiful. "Keep on living," they tell you. I wanted this sort of love, just as much as the kind that didn't end in the greater hands of fate and war and death. I even wanted the love that was a nuisance, all the way through. Mrs Edwin also met a man by the name of Danny when she was seventeen. He was the son of her local greengrocer. Whenever Mrs Edwin went in for a couple of carrots and a handful of onions, he'd tuck a paper heart into the bag with kisses marked with 'xx' in blue ink. "Danny wasn't first in the queue for good looks," she'd said to me, pushing the comment sideways out of her mouth between her story. Danny eventually asked her out, said there was a beautiful park that he knew. They could pack a picnic, he'd said – a son of a greengrocer could make delicious food. Mrs Edwin had turned him down three times before he stopped asking, but the paper hearts still made their way into her grocery bag until she moved away from her parents and never saw him again.

I wanted to be loved that much, until it became a pain to be loved that much. I think everyone would rather have options they can afford to turn down than no options at all. But there is only one type of love I would never welcome into my heart, and that is the kind that humiliates you and renders you powerless and this, I was to find, was the kind that I would take into my own hands and snuff out.

I became an agent to the humiliated, hired as a hit man or hit woman, if you will, that can erase lovers who have caused this kind of hurt. And it was Anastasia's story that had injected this sadness into me when I was young and I wanted no one else in the world to feel that pain.

The day Mrs Edwin told me about Anastasia began like any of my ordinary summer-holiday mornings. My mother made Rosemary and me some toast with a side of berries and orange juice, and my father went to work as usual. Rosemary took her journal out to the garden and I went up to the meadow where I would pick some flowers and take them to Mrs Edwin. Our houses met each other at a courtyard round the back, and in this courtyard there was an old stone fountain, the kind you see in the gardens of stately homes – double-tiered with leaf detailing around the lip, large enough for a dog to splash about in. So out of place it was. It technically belonged to Mrs Edwin and my mother didn't like me taking water from it, but I didn't listen to her. It was a particularly hot day, and after trudging my way back through the meadow with the mallow, scabious, foxglove and white campion I'd picked, my mouth had dried out and my face felt like it was a little scorched, so I set my bunch of flowers down and cupped some water from the fountain to my face. I told Mrs Edwin and said that I hoped she didn't mind. "Be very careful around that fountain, Clementine," she'd said with a sudden grave expression I'd never seen on her face before. She put the bourbon biscuit that she was about to eat back down onto her blue and pink gingham-patterned side plate and adjusted her long skirt. It was then that I noticed how engulfed her ankles were by the rest of her leg and how painful that looked; it made me understand a little more as to why she never left the house. As old as she was, she always seemed bright and happy to talk. "That fountain is very dangerous if someone is to be a fool around it," she continued. I took a pink wafer from the plate and had a sip of my tea and settled in to listen to her tale.

Before Mrs Edwin, another lady by the name of Ms Bishop had occupied the house for forty-three years. She'd told Mrs Edwin that if she were to buy the house, she must agree to never remove that fountain, or throw petals into it; she was especially never to do that. "What an odd thing to warn someone of," she'd added. My interest piqued then – I had nearly thrown petals into it. What was wrong with that? I thought it would look beautiful, little fragrant silk boats floating on the surface. Mrs Edwin said quite firmly that there was something in that fountain I wouldn't be able to see with my naked eye but was incredibly powerful, and if it ever were released, then woe betide me. I let her continue. She picked up the same biscuit again and held onto it without taking a bite as she told me that Ms Bishop had a niece by the name of Anastasia. Anastasia was a unique child. "Ms Bishop didn't mind going into unflattering detail about her niece, but I have the feeling that she was still very proud of her," Mrs Edwin said. Anastasia's mother left her with her aunt when she was four years old and ran away with a painter. Her biological father was unknown. Anastasia would wake up in the night with terrors; once she'd said that she had felt the death of an animal in the meadow. She'd begged for her aunt to go and find the hare who had just been mauled – she had felt its heart stop, Anastasia had said. With Anastasia so distressed, Ms Bishop had finally decided to go and look. She took a lantern and stepped out into the courtyard and walked across the dusty path into the meadow, where, just at the foot of it, there lay a dead hare who had in fact been mauled. Its blood was still fresh.

"These sorts of experiences grew strong, frequent and bizarre." Mrs Edwin sipped her now tepid tea and scanned my face for a reaction. I didn't give her one, but inside I was feeling like my heart already knew Anastasia. There was a sense of a kindred spirit: I was enjoying hearing about her; I could picture her clearly. I felt for her. I wanted to be her friend. Anastasia's abilities apparently went further than being able to feel the death of animals; she could also hear them. She'd said the postman's spaniel that would often accompany him on his rounds had told Anastasia his owner kicked him whenever he was frustrated. This was something Ms

Bishop insisted she keep to herself for not wanting to start trouble.

But then the more subtle 'gifts' developed, and in some ways they were more magical and more impossible to believe. Ms Bishop often caught Anastasia collecting things into a little wooden box; the items were different on different days – sometimes a key, or some soil from one of the plant pots, sometimes a scrap of fabric or a stone. She'd put the box in certain corners of the house and Ms Bishop thought it to be a treasure-hunt game of sorts – child's play. But when Ms Bishop and Anastasia bumped into friends and people they knew in town, Anastasia would give them a message such as, "Your brother and his wife will have their baby come next winter," or "Do not fret – some money is coming to you shortly." I guessed that she was psychic or that she was casting spells on people. I wasn't quite sure of the difference back then. Mrs Edwin concluded that Anastasia was a witch, which was a sentence that anchored itself into the room and could never be removed again. It also fired up my imagination. "Everything she told people came true," Mrs Edwin had said with a smile, as if she enjoyed that idea more than anything. Apparently Ms Bishop's grandmother had also possessed similar talents, and so she didn't quash Anastasia's abilities nor did she encourage them, but rather allowed them to happen. But Anastasia had to be very careful.

And I knew that tales that begin like this, told in a soft voice and with some trepidation, usually end in tragedy.

It was some years after Mrs Edwin told me about the fountain before I went back to it to summon Anastasia. I had let her story go quiet in me. When a child is told a deeply horrific story like that the fear of it mutes any outward reaction. But it is stored for all time; it is never forgotten. I would walk past the fountain and mark it, wondering if the trapped witch could hear me. Sometimes I'd whisper hello, other times I'd step a little closer and tell her small things that had happened in my day. If the water rippled, I backed off immediately and went back into my house, but I'd still keep my thoughts with her there. As I lay awake at night watching my night lamp make shadows out of my toys across the ceiling, I'd think about how frightening it was to give your heart to someone when you grew up, how confusing it was to have once believed that a person became more solid when they became an adult, but, in reality, it was quite the opposite. I'd always believed in love and had always wanted it, and that didn't change. But there was still the upsetting idea that it could take only one bad person, one person with a rotten heart, to simply destroy my healthy one. Images of Anastasia being tied to a tree haunted me for many nights and I dampened my pillow with sweat and never told my parents or Rosemary. It somehow felt too important to vocalise, and so I kept it to myself. Mrs Edwin didn't bring up Anastasia's story ever again.

I must have sobbed a few times as the nightmare came because my eyes felt sticky and puffed when I woke up. I must have watched it happen in my sleep, just as Mrs Edwin had described it: Anastasia had been forced down onto the ground by the people she'd come to trust. They were fellow teenagers she had started to call her friends. She had her hands tied together behind her back and was urinated on by the one who said he loved her. They threw rocks at her and, eventually, they hung her from a large, sturdy tree. "She'd managed to live a pretty normal life before that, despite how different she was," Mrs Edwin had recounted. "Her abilities, of course, caused her a fair bit of grief," but she had been able to make friends with people. Those who knew about her gifts kept it to themselves, and that was because she had bestowed a blessing upon them in some way. Others who didn't know about it just simply thought she was a nice young girl who was raised well by her aunt. She'd met someone, as all do, and she fell for him very quickly. He seemed to adore her too, Ms Bishop had said to Mrs Edwin. Even so many years after Anastasia's death, she still couldn't work out how he could have pretended so convincingly. When I heard the story, my first thought was that this boy, Christopher, had fallen in love with her and had adored her, until his peers told him not to.

When Mrs Edwin died, only six months after she told me this, I was left to bear the weight of things on my own. It was a small loss for my family; to them it was a shame that an old neighbour had passed away. But for me, the loss was far greater. I no longer had someone to visit and talk to. I had measured my growth and my upbringing by the days she had offered me. "Look how tall you're getting," she had said each time I had grown out of my clothes. Or she'd sometimes reminisce and say, "Remember when we spoke about my first kiss, Clementine?" I remembered it all too well, and the night she died I was the heiress to those stories and those moments, with no one else to pass them onto. They were all mine to keep, only mine.

I turned to books to push away my mourning of Mrs Edwin and the haunting of Anastasia's tale. I took comfort in reading books that were considered too childish for me, but I was well distracted by white rabbits that wore pocket watches, girls who disguised themselves as boys and treasures found in caves of wonder. At the age of fifteen my loneliness and isolation was finally appeased by a boy called Angus, who was only in town for one summer with his family. Angus also loved the meadow and was fascinated by how many flowers I could name. He had chosen me to be his friend somehow, and it continued to surprise me that he didn't make any other friends during his stay. When I spoke, he listened, and there was gravity in his brown eyes; they grounded me. He didn't have many stories to tell but he asked me to tell him plenty.

One day I confided in him about my bereavement and he took my hand when my words began to quiver in sadness. When all my tears had been shed on that gloomy afternoon, the sun broke through the clouds as if it was blasting my heaviness away; I instantly felt lighter. He kissed me then, with a tenderness that is only found in great listeners. It was my first kiss and it stayed on my lips for hours after. My mouth remained plump and I wandered around the house with that delicious secret there that tempted me to break into a smile in front of my parents. Angus and I loved each other for a full six weeks until it was time for him to go. We wrote to each other as friends for some years following until his life grew busy.

But I was hooked once more on the idea of romance. I had more reason to have faith in it after Angus, even though there were no more boys after him. When I was eighteen, my sister Rosemary announced to us that she was engaged. Rosemary and Oliver had been dating for roughly ten months by then. Rosemary was completely smitten with the tall blonde boy who had one dimple at the corner of his bright smile, and I was happy for her. Oliver did well to charm my parents; he'd asked my father for Rosemary's hand and assured my mother that he would never take her for granted. On the big day, the marquee was up in the garden, the flowers were fresh and plenty and all the guests had taken their seats, but the groom had not arrived. The violinist started to fidget. My father paced up and down the lawn; he was vexed and was tugging at his tie. My mother fiddled incessantly with Rosemary's dress, as if setting it right every ten minutes would somehow magic Oliver to her daughter's side. The guests' whispers rose from a quiet wondering into a humming speculation.

And then, finally, we all heard footsteps crunching up the gravel path and turned to see Oliver's brother, Anthony, approaching us with a distressed expression on his face. He leaned in and said something in Rosemary's ear that was inaudible to the rest of us in, but we knew he was delivering bad news. Oliver couldn't make it because he was too scared to be married. We also came to discover, after Rosemary demanded a proper explanation, that Oliver's first flame, Teresa, had returned to him and he was back in love with her. I'd never witnessed humiliation quite like that before. It was as if we could see Rosemary's heart snap into pieces just before she fell to the floor and sobbed so hard she lost her breath in a panic attack.

That night, when all the decorations had been cleared up and every last guest, performer and server had been sent home, I sat on the staircase and listened to my mother cry in my father's arms. Her wet muffled questions managed to reach my ears. "How could he do this to her? How will she get over this? How do we help to mend our poor baby's heart?" I was reminded of Anastasia's broken heart, kicked and smashed by a group of people who wanted to ridicule her, and then murdered by Christopher, who was too weak to admit he loved her. It was all so terrifying, cruel and unfair. I became seriously angry, and before I knew it, I was tearing out the petals from my bridesmaid bouquet of freesias and was running to the stone fountain. I wanted to summon Anastasia; I believed that if I brought her back to life, she could fix everything.

The wind rose up and swirled in the air as I threw the petals into the fountain and called Anastasia by her name. A sweet and heady floral fragrance permeated the stagnant summer air around me. The water rippled the way I imagine the ground to tremor in the aftershocks of an earthquake. I heard whispers back, but couldn't decipher the words, and so I spoke louder. I asked her to awaken from her hundred-year-long imprisonment. I had come to set her free, I needed her, we could work together to put things right. I knew she could hear me.

I jumped back when I caught sight of fingers in the moonlight, clutching at the rim of the fountain. Then her head rose up, a mass of hair floating up through the surface of the water, and then came the other hand, and suddenly her face met mine as she stood and opened her eyes. I felt a thunderbolt through me when I took in her beauty. The moon and the lights coming from my home illuminated her face in an ethereal glow. I had always assumed death to be such an ugly thing, but Anastasia had managed to defy it. She was more like a water nymph than a witch; youth was still in her skin. She held out a cold, wet hand to me and I took it in mine and helped her out onto the ground. There was a moment where I thought she might harm me. She had just risen from death and she'd been so wronged when alive that she could have lashed out at anyone. But instead, she pulled me into her for an embrace. I felt that love for her again; after all, I had already fallen for her when I was a child.

I snuck her into my room, found a towel for her to dry herself off with, and told her that I'd need to find a way of introducing her to my parents. "Tell them that I'm an old friend from school who moved away but I'm back and I need a place to stay for a while," she suggested. I didn't think my parents knew that I had no friends at school – they had never asked about it – and so I agreed. But it was strange that I felt that this was exactly who she was to me. Looking at her felt like I was looking at an old friend who was back with me. We were together again; I knew her, I truly did. Even her almond-shaped brown eyes seemed familiar to me. She sat on the edge of my bed with my old teddy bear in her arms and looked around at my room and smiled whenever she saw some-thing about it that she liked. She thanked me for freeing her and then asked me why I had done it. I explained everything to her, and Anastasia's jaws clenched with anger when I told her about what had happened to my sister.

"I want to punish him and heal her broken heart. Is there a spell you could do for that?" I asked her. Despite Rosemary never paying much mind to me, I thought that if I could change things for her and make her happier in some way and get rid of the man who had hurt her, the magic might also bring her closer to me.

Anastasia breathed ancient words that I couldn't understand into a single white orchid. The orchid was sent to Oliver with no card attached, for this would be too risky. He must have accepted, believing it was a belated wedding gift from a sender who hadn't heard about the cancellation, or a peace offering from Rosemary, letting him know all was forgiven. Oliver was found dead that same day, slumped against the bottom of the staircase in his hallway. The orchid sat all beautiful and innocent on a side table by a coat stand. There was some speculation that Oliver had poisoned himself to death after fully realising how much he'd hurt Rosemary. I was worried we had done the wrong thing when Rosemary received the news, not because we'd committed murder, but because the news of his death deepened her agony. She still loved him and the belief that he might have performed an act of self-punishment gave him back his previously respectable reputation. Anastasia prepared a soup for Rosemary to eat that would cause her to mend rapidly, and, even better, feel nothing for Oliver anymore. I brought the broth to boil and carried it up to Rosemary, who had stayed in bed since the day of her wedding.

It had been three days. This had been the only time Rosemary let me spend time with her. I sat in her bed and tickled her toes to cheer her up, and she giggled with me for the first time. For the actual spell itself, Anastasia used some plants and flowers from the meadow and instructed me to go to the market for the rest. Anastasia tied a piece of rope around a photo of Rosemary and Oliver that I had taken from Rosemary's bedroom when she was asleep. She then sliced it through the middle with a knife and put one half in a box that she buried on the front lawn and the other she buried in the back garden. She stood at each and chanted with her eyes closed and seemed to breathe in a force that I couldn't see. Not long after that, Rosemary moved away to Paris and took up a degree in fine arts. She has made new friends and she often writes letters to my parents in happy tones.

My friend Anastasia and I moved to the city together within weeks of that first spell and decided we would set up an agency. I had developed a real rush and sense of purpose from having sent the deadly orchid to Oliver and I wanted to do it again. Anastasia was adjusting to a world she didn't recognise anymore, and the two of us grew together. We were a perfect team. We started discreetly handing out business cards to women we found at parties and in tearooms. Anastasia used her gifts to pick out the ones who were in strife. We'd befriend these women and then slip them a little black card with the words "Bella Donna Floristry and Other Services" printed on it in silver ink. Anastasia's intuition could also tell us who would keep the details of Bella Donna to themselves. After all, these women had no one else to turn to and I understood that feeling. Eventually, men started to approach us too. After all, every human being can suffer because of love. It isn't about gender, but about a fragile organ that we all carry in our chests.

Our second client, who asked us to send pink carnations to his girlfriend, was so distressed by her sleeping with his father that he wanted to send a bunch to his father as well and to everyone he knew, as if to erase all the people in his life and therefore to erase himself. Anastasia sat with him in our office and took his hand in hers. Without words, she managed to calm his angry mind. He took a deep breath and concurred that karma would get his father someday. No matter how much pain he wanted to inflict on his father, he still couldn't see him dead. I reminded him that we could only send one bunch per client.

How my soft and open heart has changed into a heavy one since I was twelve years old. I look at the piles of envelopes on my desk now. There are stacks of sorrowful letters, which I read carefully every day from people pleading for my help; I can almost feel their tears through their words. The most recent case Anastasia and I dealt with was of a girl whose father sold her to a business partner. She'd told us of how she was taken to this man's house the minute she turned eighteen, how he'd knot ropes around her ankles and wrists and put her into a position similar to that of a spit-roast pig. He'd enter her viciously and she'd cry until her eyes stung and blinded her while her father enjoyed the handsome payments for her as they flowed swiftly into his bank account. The flowers she'd asked us to send were not for her perverse owner but for her father, delivered under the pretence that he had his own secret admirer, something he'd never experienced in all the eight years since his wife had died. "I'll find my own way to deal with my disgusting bedfellow," the girl had written confidently. "But get the bastard who was supposed to love me and protect me." This situation particularly got to us. As Anastasia and I discussed it, I couldn't help but feel the sickness mount up in me, thinking about what was happening to this poor girl now, and how her father could be out there, feeling completely fine with what he had done. I chose the bouquet and Anastasia cast her deadly spell. From what I understand, his bunch of indigo hydrangeas arrived safely, were signed for by himself. Later that day, he'd been found by the next-door neighbour, cold, stiff and blue – just as his heart had been when he'd lived. It was pronounced as death by stroke, put down to work stress. I received a note with just the words "thank you" inked on the paper, in the very same handwriting of that poor, dear girl.

It used to feel good doing this. Ever since the very first case, I believed that I was taking control of the universe in some way, that I could justify it. I've felt at peace knowing that I have managed to erase dark hearts from this world. But it is hard for me to admit that something very grave is happening inside me these days, and I worry about what is to come of this. I look over at Anastasia now. She has fallen asleep in the armchair by the fireplace, her long hair fanning out across her shoulders and over her arms like vines spreading across a stone wall. Her small peach mouth is sealed shut, her cheeks are soft and still, her face is relaxed, and I hope this is how she looked when she had died, hanging from that tree. I hope her soul left her blissfully and was kind enough to put the body completely at rest first. Her black eyelashes flutter now; she is dreaming. One of her small pink fingers twitches and it is as if it is attached to a string that controls my heart, because it flutters in response.

We've been doing this for a year now; so far we haven't been caught. We've put a lot of lives right, but I no longer carry the same venom for heartbreakers in the way I used to. Perhaps it is because I am no longer lonely and my own heart is too full of love. I have started to think about what it would be like to just be with Anastasia - no plans, no schemes, no spells; just the two of us, sharing a life. Would that work? Would I be happy? I shake these thoughts off and push the envelopes away on the desk. I cannot work for the moment. I leave our office in the attic and climb down the wooden stairs to our apartment. It is modestly sized, but it is a warm place, full of paintings and flowers of our own which we've collected from markets - these flowers I cherish, for they are not deadly. I lean in to inhale the scent of the pink peonies sitting in an oyster-coloured vase; they are my favourite. The scent of them brings to me the image of baby powder dusted over young, feminine skin that has been soaked in luxurious bath oils. I sometimes miss picking bunches in the meadow and bringing them to Mrs Edwin. I miss her, too. I still cannot make new friends because it is dangerous for anyone other than clients to know what we do. It also means that if I do make acquaintances, I must lie to them about what my life is like, and I hate doing that.

The living room is pitch dark. The autumn has truly set our clocks askew; the sun abandons us so early these days. It is only four in the afternoon and later Anastasia and I will have dinner together and read books side by side on the sofa, and then we will bathe and tuck ourselves into the bed we share, just like every evening. We like talking late at night so much that we decided that we should just share a bed instead of buying another; we'd only creep into each other's room anyway. We talk about what the rest of the world might be like in, say for instance, Japan or Argentina. I listen to her tell me what the world was like when she was alive. I hate to admit it, but I choose to forget that she is undead. She is a ghost truthfully, and even though her blood is flowing just like mine, I am acquainting myself with something unearthly and deranged. But then she puts a warm arm on mine when she tells me what life was like back then: "No cars, no telephones. There was no way of escaping and no way of reaching out to someone, Clementine!" And that touch, and those choco-late-coloured eyes, inject more life into me than the sun or any scent of a flower. But still, I am thinking of friends I could have had, thrills I could have experienced, like Rosemary is now in Paris. My parents do not visit; I cannot risk it, and it makes me too sad to go up and see them in the country. Nature has too strong a hold on me – it sends me into reveries and wistfulness and that is what drove me to attach myself to the idea of Anastasia in the first place. In the city, I am sharp, clear and ruthless with what I cannot afford to keep, and that includes normal human relationships. But I still despair.

I am restless for the next few nights. That dark feeling in me has caused me to lose sleep. Anastasia doesn't stir when I toss and turn and sit up trying to work out what bad omens I am sensing. On the third night of this, I wrap my night robe around me to keep off the early-morning chill and head up to the office and open some of the letters I have been putting off. I don't switch the light on, as it feels too harsh to do so; instead, I light a candle at my desk. I go through each letter: A man who has seen his wife going into another man's house is convinced she is cheating on him and would like us to send her a bunch of roses as if from her lover. A young girl has found us through her school friend's older sister whom she overheard discussing her own situation and would like us to send a bunch to her mother because she believes her mother does not love her. She is offering to pay us with the contents of her coin jar that she has been saving up for two years. I have finally reached a point where I believe Bella Donna cannot help people anymore. How could I possibly have a young girl's mother killed? More to the issue, what illness is in such a young girl that she wants to commit murder? We cannot cast spells for those who temporarily cannot see clearly, who are not seeing the full consequences of their desires. For Oliver, I didn't feel remorse; he'd hurt and humiliated my sister. For the father who sold his daughter to a business partner, I most certainly do not feel remorse. Nor for all the others who seemed to know what harms they were causing but didn't care. But for this young girl's mother, it is not right. Some authority needs to investigate this, not a witch. I open the third letter in my lap and when I draw it up close in the light of my candle, a name lurches off the paper and plummets into my stomach. Angus. Is it my Angus? My childhood summer sweetheart? My dear, shy friend who kissed me so tenderly all those years ago?

I read it carefully. It is from a woman named Alice who says that she is in agony because a man named Angus Kingsley will not return her love. I tremble at reading the full name – it is him. She has tried to win his heart for some months but he says that his mind is on someone else. She is hurt and refuses to believe that he doesn't love her; he just doesn't want to. Perhaps it is because of my bias for Angus that I feel this Alice woman is manic; her explanations to me seem fickle and unjustified. The bottom line is, she wants him dead. I cannot abide this. I won't do it, and I will not let Anastasia do it. How could someone be so cruel as to dispel of someone kind and sweet like Angus, who cannot help whom he loves? And at this thought I get a wave of sickness up my throat. People cannot help whom they love and sometimes they don't know how to go about it. Perhaps we have made wrong choices in agreeing to some of our clients' business. I never expected to be asked to kill someone I know, someone I hold dear to me, and I wonder if Anastasia will agree that this shouldn't be done.

I hear the wooden stairs creak - she is awake. When she appears at the door, the sickness subsides; I can't help but think she is lovely. I believe she wouldn't do anything to harm or upset me. She loves me, I know that she does. Look how she smiles at me now. Her smile is dripping with honey sweetness; her face softens when her lips spread wide to show me her tenderness. "What are you doing up?" she asks me and wafts into the room like a warm, tropical breeze, her long bed-tousled hair fluttering a little as she moves, her cream night gown swaying. But then it's as if a cloud skims across her face when she sees the horror in mine. Her smile drops and a shadow falls. "What's the matter, Clementine?" I show her the letter and once she's read it, she looks at me expectantly for me to elaborate. "I don't understand," she says, her voice cutting through the silence I've held in as if I'm holding my breath underwater.

"He was my first love," I respond. She nods and looks back down at the letter, now understanding everything she needs to. "We can't do this one," I continue.

"Why not?" she asks me, and in return I ask her to hear the

words Alice has written. "Doesn't she sound unreasonable?" My exasperation nearly blows out the candle; it wavers and then regains its teardrop form.

"She's in despair, just like all our clients. If we turn our back on her, we turn our back on them all," she tells me, and places the letter onto my desk and folds her arms; I have annoyed her.

"Can't you see this is different?" I cannot believe that she doesn't understand this, that Angus has done nothing wrong.

"When did we start looking at cases differently, Clementine? We run an agency. We agreed to do one thing and one thing only: respond to clients with their one wish." Anastasia takes a seat in the armchair she is so fond of and looks at the fireplace as if she wants to light it. It is cold in here; I feel chills bouncing up and down my spine and across my shoulders.

"He hasn't done anything wrong from what I've read here. Aren't we bound to come across a client who isn't of sound mind? Aren't we supposed to recognise that and do the right thing?" I'm suddenly aware that I am crying now; my throat is warbling and the tears are being pushed out of my eyes as if by some force other than myself. They stream down my cheeks and drip onto the desk. Anastasia's eyes slip from defiance into sympathy. She rushes over to me, she strokes my hair and cradles my head in her arms.

"Don't cry, my darling Clementine. Don't cry." Her lips kiss my crown and instantly I feel heavy and ready to sleep again.

After being back in bed for several hours, I am startled awake by the telephone. Anastasia muttered something about heading out to the market when I crawled back under the bedding at nearly six o'clock; I was too tired to continue our discussion about Angus. The telephone call comes from my mother, who asks me to take the next train home if I can – my father is suddenly very ill and she doesn't know if he can pull through. I pack some clothes and toiletries as quickly as I can. I write Anastasia a note and leave for Paddington.

It is strange to be back in my childhood home. The first thing I do as I walk up the gravel path and look over at the house that used to be Mrs Edwin's, and I am sad to tell myself she is not in there, putting biscuits onto a plate and adjusting her beloved photos in their frames. I head to the back courtyard and look at the fountain that used to move and whisper to me. It is silent and still; it is dead. The soul that used to keep it alive left it to be with me; it had been my turn to be kept alive. The yellow curtains in Mrs Edwin's back windows are still there. Mrs Edwin's sister had come to deal with her affairs when she passed away but never planned to move into the house and didn't seem to want to sell it either, so it had been abandoned. I should be concerned with my father's illness but I am disturbed by my last discussion with Anastasia, I am plagued by what I had read in Alice's letter. I go inside my parents' home and no one is there, but my mother has left me a note – she is at the hospital waiting for me. I set my things down in my old room and head straight back out to the meadow to see what I can find to pick at this time of the year. Perhaps there are dahlias. A bunch of flowers would cheer my family a little; it would bring me back to my old world.

My anxiety grows over the next few days. My father takes a turn for the worse, and my sister Rosemary arrives from

Paris looking pale and skinny, with dark clouds under eyes. She is tired; she has been busy living. I find myself feeling jealous. She tells me a few stories of a best friend she's made named Sylvie and someone called Thierry who has taken her out dancing a few times. And yet even as she does this, and even as our family is in crisis, she still does not embrace me; I don't think she has missed me at all. We take it in turns to go and visit my father, and one morning while my mother and Rosemary are at the hospital, I walk around the house, I go to the meadow, and I come back and sit by the fountain as if I'm retracing my steps back to the point where I went wrong in life, so that I can go forwards again the correct way. I decide to clean the kitchen, which has been abandoned for some days. My mother would be grateful for the help. I wash the dishes, tidy away tins and cereal boxes left on the table, I wipe down the counters, dust the overhanging copper pots, and while I work a dust cloth into the depths of a large saucepan, I hit something and it falls off a hook, jingling as it drops. I look down past the stool I am standing on and to the floor to find a bunch of keys with a yellow tag attached. I step down, pick them up, and remember that this is a spare set to Mrs Edwin's house. She had given them to us, just in case we ever needed them. I throw the cloth down into the sink and grab my coat from the peg by the door and head over to the house I haven't stepped in for so long.

I want to just be in there again, to see her things, recall her stories, her smell of dusting powder and honeysuckle, her biscuits and her teacups. I want to feel small again, sitting in that cramped and cluttered living room. Everything in it was part of a collection that she never would have thrown away:

ornaments of animals, bells, novelty clocks and little women in milkmaid dresses – she said that her sister once lived in Holland. The lemon wallpaper has curled a little now at the seams. Everything is in some shade of her favourite colour, yellow. I think of sherbet, sunshine, summer dresses and sunflowers; a summer that never ends resides in this house. I also realise now that I never went upstairs. I never really saw what was up there. I imagine more of the same trinkets and keepsakes in her bedroom, but I still wish to see it. My steps are silent going up the carpeted staircase. The smell of powder is still here and it thickens as I ascend – perhaps it is dust and age.

The bedroom is as I suspected; I smile at its predictability. Lemon bedspread, another novelty clock in the shape of a windmill, three clay cats on the windowsill and a bookcase filled with some novels I recognise, some poetry, some world maps and a few torn cloth-bound volumes of something with no title. I pull one of these out and open it; as I free it, the trapped scent of musk jumps up my nostrils. Some leaves are coming loose from the spine and so I sit down on the bed and hold the book carefully. The ink writing is very old and blurred and quite difficult to read, but soon enough I grasp that this is a book of witchcraft and spells. Outside I hear an engine running and tyres crunching across the gravel; my mother and Rosemary are home from the hospital. I take the book with me, lock the house up and enter my parents' home from the back door, hooking Mrs Edwin's keys back up under the copper pots. My mother and sister enter the house just as I turn at the top of the stairs to put the book of spells in my room.

When I come back downstairs, my mother is filling up the kettle and Rosemary is leafing through the post. She soon loses interest and throws the letters onto the table without handing any over. My mother tells me that the nurses insisted they come back and get some rest, but my father is showing signs of an infection and they will phone us should anything happen. "Guess who I bumped into at the hospital?" my mother says, her mouth lazy with fatigue. "Do you remember that family that was here one summer, the Kingstons or Kingsleys?" I lose my breath. "They lost their son, Angus, two days ago. You two were friends weren't you?" My chest heaves and the tears are choking me as I do my best to hold them in; the contents of my stomach threaten to evacuate through my mouth. My mother continues talking, but I only hear the words "such a shame", "not sure why they were back here." Rosemary is the one to notice that I look sick.

"Are you all right, Clementine?" I manage to whisper that I am in shock; but I am beyond shock – there is sickness and pain and the stab of deep betrayal. I cannot believe Anastasia went through with it; I cannot believe she killed Angus.

Anastasia arrives that afternoon; she says she has come to give me support. After a deeply tragic afternoon of coping with the news and watching my father's flesh sink down to his bones in the hospital, I came home to find her on our doorstep with the carpet bag she bought in one of the markets she likes to visit. I despise her in this moment, but I cannot stop looking at her. My heart will never want to stop looking at her.

But I have already figured out how to handle this situation. I will gain back control of my life. The book of spells I found at Mrs Edwin's told me how.

We fight at first, of course; I cannot contain how angry I am and I tell her that I'm quitting Bella Donna. She begs me to rethink things, she pleads with me that she had done the right thing and we had gone into this business to help people. "I helped Alice like she asked us to," Anastasia says. She keeps trying to advance towards me as I pace up and down my bedroom. "We live together, we share a life together," she says to me, and although this is simple fact, the way she says it tells me that it means more to her than I have realised. It means exactly what I used to hope it meant. I tell her I can't bear it, that my mourning for an innocent, sweet and dear old friend will never stop. She has ruined things. As soon as I tell her so, she launches herself at me. At first I think she will wrap her hands around my throat, but instead she pushes her tongue into my mouth and we kiss until my body is drained of all energy to resist.

With the taste of her still in my mouth and the heat of her skin still on mine, I leave her in my bed, go downstairs and snatch from the vase in the hallway the extra dahlias I had picked the other morning. I take some candles from the side table there and head out to the fountain. I set some flowers at the base and scatter petals on the surface of the water. The spell book says that to cast Anastasia back into the world where the dead belong, I must give her a funeral in the exact spot where she was resurrected. I have to give Anastasia the goodbye she never had. Flower petals must be thrown in as before, but I am to chant her back to the grave and wish her soul to rest. I guess that this was a book left to Mrs Edwin by Ms Bishop. It is one that Ms Bishop seems to have written herself; all of it is about Anastasia, the unfortunate witch. It seems that the tree where Anastasia was hanged was ripped down and then the fountain was built in its place. Hauntings were documented in the book; there was a note about hearing Anastasia's voice coming from under the water. In the loss of her niece, Ms Bishop had researched her family's heritage of witchcraft, had read books on rituals and had figured out how to raise her back from the dead and then put her back again. It is strange what grief and loss will make us do.

I light the candles and begin to sing the only mournful song I can think of in that moment: "Nearer, My God to Thee," a funeral hymn. I'm not really sure how I know it, but there the words are, trembling out from my lips, the tune soaked in sorrow. I am weeping for my dearest Anastasia who I call to me now so I can lay her to rest. And sure enough, she comes. Just like the first night I saw her, her eyes startle me and my chest grows hot and short of breath. On that first night I bid her welcome, and with the way she is looking at me now, she can tell that I am saying goodbye.

"Why are you doing this, Clementine?" she asks. I continue to sing. "Stop it, Clementine, stop it." The tears drip from my chin and onto my chest, the words of the hymn getting thinner from my melancholy. "Don't you love me, Clementine?" I come to the end of the verse. Anastasia crouches down to look at the flowers around the fountain and her eyes catch the reflection of the candle flames.

"It's time for you to rest, my dearest love," I say to her, sobbing.

"No, Clementine." She comes over and clings to me, holds me tight and cries into me. "No Clementine. You mean everything to me, please don't make me go." I try to tell her that she cannot be amongst the living anymore. Our purpose together is over; the danger of her spells must end now. My words are twisted when they come out, but she understands what it is that I am trying to say.

"I need you, Clementine!" she begins to scream. Her dark hair, which I loved to watch spread over her shoulders, is now stringy and damp with sweat and tears.

"I send you back, Anastasia the witch. I send you back to your resting place. I cast your soul into the light where you may find peace," I begin. She tries to stop me, but I carry on and repeat my words until she is torn away from me and is stepping backwards towards the fountain. "Go now, go to the realm of spirit where you belong. I cast you from this world." I can see her struggle, fighting the force that drags her feet along the gravel; her toes curl as if to grip the ground beneath her, but she cannot stop this. She clutches the rim of the fountain like a child who refuses to be torn from her mother. "With great love, I send you peace. Go now, witch." She steps into the water, still begging me to stop. The spell is nearly over; the wind picks up and the water in the fountain begins with a ripple and then bubbles with an eagerness to pull her in. "I send you back, Anastasia. I cast your soul into the light where you may find peace." Anastasia screams my name one last time and the echo of it rings through the air after she disappears.

The most important condition of that spell was that the one to perform it must have a broken heart, someone who could empathise with Anastasia's pain. And then I realised that this is what I have been feeling for a while. That haunting sense of something bad to come, that heaviness that woke me in the night – it was my heart breaking. I had fallen in love, knowing that I would have to let go of it.

I stand for some time watching the water settle and the large wild flames of the candles shrink to steadiness. I hear the phone ringing from inside the house and I run to it. It is Rosemary with sad news. As Anastasia's soul was sent to where it belongs, my father's has left this world too. Tonight there were not two deaths, but three: Anastasia, my father and my heart. But as Anastasia proved to me, there is an afterlife, another world and another time, so I know that my heart can be born again and find that faith in love that I had when I was a child – when I was picking my flowers and breathing in the glorious perfume of life.

The Earth-Bound Express

A T THE END of the tunnel of light, Dahlia finds herself
standing on a train platform. This platform is essentially
a single rickety old wooden stage in the middle of nowhere.
There is no shelter, no awning, no ticket machines or staff; it
is a railroad platform built just for boarding. No loved ones
waiting for passengers to arrive, no travellers loitering and
exploring. The sunshine is bright and the land around her is
vast. She thinks it looks like the plains of Oklahoma, where
fields of corn sway back and forth in a light warm breeze,
jade-coloured hills in the far distance cradle the blue sky, and
the white-noise-like sound of cicadas fills the silence. Except
here there is no breeze and no sound; the air is deadly quiet
and eerily still. Dahlia does not feel warm. She wonders what
she is waiting for, here on this platform. If it is a train, when
will it come? And where will it take her? She thinks about
where she was just moments before. She was with John. And
then, she remembers, that he said he would follow her if she
ever died, he would follow her straight away.

He'd told her that once before on a night similar to the one
she'd just come from. When the drugs were rushing through
her like white-water rapids in her veins, when she'd enjoyed
it, then hated it and cried on the kitchen floor, curled into a
ball, waiting for John to stroke her to sleep. He'd carried her
to their mattress on the floor of their studio apartment, told
their other friends they needed to leave, which wasn't well

received. "Not our fault she can't hold down her medicine," Eddie had said.

"Just find another hole to crawl into," John's cracked voice had replied. He'd tried not to sound worried, but he was. He breathed heavily when he got into bed with her; he was still rushing but he seemed lucid. The record player was still spinning Lou Reed's voice slowly round and the flames of the pillar candles that were sitting in the corners of the room were dwindling. Darkness was coming.

"What if I die like this, Johnnie?" she'd managed to say, but the words seemed to seep out of her mouth like drool.

"Then I'd join you, I'd be there right behind you," he had replied. He'd repeated it twice just to make sure she knew. The next day she had woken up and remembered it, but this time she didn't wake up next to him.

"You know you've died, don't you, child?" A thick, sweet voice pours into her right ear. Dahlia turns and sees a woman standing next to her on the platform. Her eyes are hazel; they look like acorns that have been set in amber resin. Her skin is the colour of hazelnut, and her thick black hair is straight and braided neatly into two plaits. She is beautiful and the softness radiating from her presence makes Dahlia feel like she will be OK.

Dahlia nods and replies, "I do know. I was expecting it to happen sometime soon anyway." That is an odd thing for a young person to say, the woman thinks, but it means that Dahlia had known, she'd felt her life coming to completion.

"There's a train coming for you. You'll be taking that to the next life," her honey-soaked voice says.

"I'm waiting for John. He'll be coming with me. He'll be along soon." Dahlia looks behind her, expecting to see the tunnel she'd emerged from, but there is nothing, just more golden plains. The woman tilts her head gently as if to get a better look into Dahlia's eyes, and smiles.

"You'll be getting on that train, Dahlia. But before you do, I want you to tell me what it is you were supposed to bring back to me from your time on earth?" Dahlia is confused and frowns to indicate so. "Before you were born into that world, you were right here with me before. I asked you to bring something back. That was your purpose." Dahlia doesn't remember yet that she has met this woman before and that her name is Leonie.

She doesn't remember yet that she been here before, four times to be exact. And at the end of each life, just before the next, she promises Leonie that she will bring something back. If she fails, she goes straight back to the world she thinks is her home.

A word comes to her suddenly, as if given to her: "Belief?"

Leonie nods. "You didn't manage to believe. You didn't believe in yourself and you didn't believe enough in others. You didn't truly believe in things being good and whole and correct." Leonie's voice remains soft as she tells Dahlia this, but Dahlia can't help but feel she is being reprimanded, a child who knows she has done wrong.

"I know I did some terrible things. If my parents had been alive they'd have been so disappointed in me, I know that. I didn't want to escape through drugs and ignorance, but I was too scared to be sober, to have my eyes wide open. I was too afraid of what I'd see." Dahlia wants to cry, but there are no tears to fall; she no longer possesses a body that can do so, but she can feel the crying in her soul.

"You saw John," Leonie says.

"Yes, John, the only person who truly makes me feel safe and who loves me so much. He'll be coming soon, he will." Dahlia looks once more around her. The scene has not moved, a cloud hasn't floated by, the grass does not sway; it is a 3-D picture, completely stuck. "Where are my parents? Will I see them?" Dahlia thinks of the sad ways in which they passed: her mother developed cancer, and when she deteriorated quickly into nothingness, her father couldn't go on. Dying of a broken heart – it wasn't common, but it happened. She wonders if they would recognise her now. She isn't that nine-year-old girl anymore in her tea dress and pretty shoes, she is twenty, or was, up until just minutes ago. She is wearing a thin, worn T-shirt and a thrift-store skirt. Her hair is thick and unbrushed and she is barefooted, her toe nails painted an autumn orange. 'Organic' might've been how Dahlia would have described herself before, but now she thinks she is a mess and always has been. Leonie shakes her head slowly and looks straight ahead as she explains to Dahlia that her parents are both back in different lives with different purposes.

"The only folks you'll find on the train are the ones who are between lives," she explains.

Past the top of Leonie's head, Dahlia sees a puff of steam in the distance. The tracks begin to vibrate, and for the first time in this tableau, Dahlia can see movement. The sound of a steam train's whistle hoots and jolts her a little. The train is coming and Dahlia begins to panic – John is not here yet. The train comes in slowly, and it is beautiful, looking like something from a Victorian postcard. Dahlia has never been on a train that looks like this. She can only recall too well the stuffiness, the grime, and the oppression of subway trains in New York whenever she went to visit her uncle Larry. She can only think of the miserable faces riding them and the sicknesses they carried. The train halts and a single door on the carriage in front of them opens, as if by itself. "Go on now, Dahlia, it's time for you to board." Leonie places a hand on the small of Dahlia's back to encourage her forward. The sensation of the woman's palm gives Dahlia a rush, much like the drug she had come to depend on for the feeling of golden warmth, like being washed over with liquid sunshine. Dahlia has so many more questions to ask Leonie, but she cannot get them out. She needs to wait for John. Leonie pushes her gently forward and the whistle hoots once more, causing her to start onto the steps of the carriage.

"Where do I get off?" Dahlia manages to ask, but the door shuts behind her and through the window Leonie smiles, waves once, and disappears.

The train makes a hiss, as if scowling at the one forcing it to move. The wheels take a while to get going, but soon enough Dahlia is being taken away. The train picks up a motion that judders before it gains speed, and Dahlia hangs on to her balance by placing her hand on the carriage wall. The carriage smells like old soft leather and Earl Grey tea. Most of the seats are empty, but over at the far end, double seats face each other and there sit groups of people talking and drinking from china cups. Dahlia is relieved to see that ghosts can smell and taste. A man with a trolley enters the carriage behind her. He is tall, stooping down over his wonderfully colourful cakes and teapots; his blonde hair is combed slickly over from a neat side parting and he wears a blue waistcoat and a brown shirt. His large blue eyes and tidy features suggest to Dahlia that he is perhaps German or Swedish, maybe Austrian. "Please take a seat, miss," he says to Dahlia firmly, but softens it with a smile. His accent isn't quite English, but surely European. Dahlia walks forward, hoping that John is on this train; perhaps he has come through from a different place. Pale faces look up at her. No one here carries the colour in their cheeks or glow in the skin that is reserved for the living. Dahlia decides to sit in the empty window seat, one space away from a woman who looks to be in her forties. She has a mother's face, tired but kind. She wears a billowy, bright, white and pink dress; her hair is thick and wavy, pinned up smartly on either side. Dahlia vaguely remembers this look being in all the fashion magazines when she was just a small girl.

The scenery is whizzing by outside the windows and remains very much the same as it was where Dahlia boarded. There is nothing interesting for her to look at and so, in a discreet sideways glance, she inspects the other passengers sitting adjacent as the server pulls up alongside them with his trolley. There are two men and two women. One of the men has thick fluffy white hair and a moustache to match; he wears a brown suit that seems older than he would like it to be. He has had a long life, Dahlia can tell, and he looks around him gently as if the action of taking things in tires him. He takes a steaming cup from the server and holds it close to his chest. He is pensive, quiet, and seems to just be holding onto something, waiting, much like Dahlia maybe, for that special person to light him up again. The woman sat facing him wears clothes too extravagant for a place like this, even too elegant for the time Dahlia is from, where dresses hang low enough to brush the ankles and T-shirts are worn with comfort and convenience. This woman is held in by a bodice, and her silk, blue, pastel gown threatens to pop her breasts at the neckline. Dahlia and many of the women of her generation abandon bras in an act of liberation. Camisoles hang loose and straps slip; nakedness is suggested. Dahlia admires the woman's golden coiffed hair: it is curled so neatly and tucked in with so many invisible pins that it does not move as she shakes her head at the cakes being offered to her. She sips her tea stiffly, holding in her breath tight. Her face seems to be powdered as it retains a chalkiness that her delicate fingers do not possess. She never makes eye contact with her fellow passengers. The woman sitting next to her is a woman whom Dahlia has no doubt is Native American; she seems young, although not as young as Dahlia. Her face is not worn with tiredness like the others. Her brown eyes are bright and searching, but for what Dahlia does not know. Dahlia senses that this woman will not speak to a soul on this journey.

The server cuts a piece of a chocolate cake with two layers, places it carefully on a pretty plate, and hands it along with a silver dessert fork to the smart man in an army uniform. Dahlia isn't sure of which army and doesn't recognise from which time this man has come, but he was certainly an officer. His dark hair is thin and short and slicked neatly at the sides. He is clean-shaven, his thin lips are pressed together as if he is holding his speech in: there are things he does not want to say to anyone. He straightens his uniform jacket before he takes a bite from the cake and he dabs at the corners of his mouth with a handkerchief he produces from his pocket. Dahlia wonders just how long these people have been on this train and how long she will be here, waiting. The server then turns to the woman closest to Dahlia, the fifties' wife or mother in the pink and white dress, who asks for a cup of coffee. "I have Brazilian, Columbian, French, Arabic – well, just about any roast you'd like. You make your choice," the server says, and he smiles then, a genuine smile that softens his Anglo features.

"French this time please, Erik." Her voice is polite and warm, and Dahlia thinks of her mother then. She might have had a dress like that. There are many things Dahlia cannot remember about her mother, but her voice, much like this woman's, still swirls gently around in the air around her. The smell of the coffee arouses Dahlia's desire for one herself, and when Erik turns to her, holding the pot up, Dahlia tells him that she'll have the same. To Dahlia, holding a fresh cup of coffee is like holding in your hands fresh hope for the day. The smell of it, and that first sip, was always how she greeted her mornings. The day ahead was promising in these moments; nothing had yet gone wrong and she was allowed to erase what happened the day before.

She rests and thinks on of more good memories and then starts with panic when the bad ones sneak in. In her good memories she is eight years old and dancing to records with her mother. She is fourteen years old and on a trip to San Diego with her best friend, Joni, and her family. She is eighteen and meeting John for the first time at a concert. The bad memories contain the loss of all of these things. John has not followed her. He said he would – how long will he be? Dahlia decides to get up and move around the train to see if he is there. She is also very restless and wishes to know who else might be here and what the other carriages hold. Not a single one of her fellow passengers has spoken to her directly yet, and she is not sure if she is grateful for that or not, but she wonders if there is a silent, mutual feeling between them all. They are sharing their death and this train, but perhaps they also share the same losses and yearnings, and to vocalise them to one another would just make these feelings more real. And although they may not be able to experience physical pain anymore, there is still a hurt that can be felt, right in the core of their spirits.

After her coffee and slice of tiramisu – a small comfort – Dahlia decides to wander through the train. When she crosses into the next carriage, she instantly feels a change in the air. It is livelier here; it is warmer. General chatter flutters down the aisle like butterflies. Dahlia feels like she has just stepped into a dinner party, and if there was music playing, it would be jazz, something from the thirties like Cab Calloway – the kind of music her father appreciated. This carriage smells of faint cigarette smoke, rum, and something sweetly floral like jasmine. She wonders if she can get a cigarette here. Dahlia passes a child wearing a rag of a dress who is playing cat's cradle with a teenage girl who is wearing a black slip dress and red lipstick. She glances up at Dahlia and smiles a smile that is something between friendliness and flirtation; an expression, it seems, that she has used often. A male in possibly his mid-thirties is eating a piece of apple pie with such relish that his eyes are entirely focused on his plate and do not look around him. An old African woman hobbles out of her seat and heads towards the other adjoining door away from

Dahlia. Two middle-aged men are speaking emphatically to each other in French. One is dressed in a smart jacket in a style reminiscent of the 1600s and the other is dressed in a simple white shirt, his hair is in a small ponytail.

"I know you!" Dahlia suddenly hears a jolly female voice, and when she looks for its owner, she realises that this woman is talking to her. She looks at Dahlia with delighted recognition. Dahlia does not recognise her. "Don't you remember? You're from my life before my last!" the cheerful woman exclaims. Then she leans towards the woman sitting opposite her who wears a black Victorian dress and a bronze flower in her hair and says to her, "This is my best friend from the 1800s!" The woman shuffles over in her seat and indicates for Dahlia to sit down. "Did you just get here?" The woman who knows Dahlia has a bright face and watery blue eyes and Dahlia wonders if she died smiling like this.

"Yes, I'm not really sure what I'm supposed to be doing," Dahlia replies and looks some more at the same scenery out the window, feeling too nervous to discuss herself with someone who seems to know everything that she doesn't.

"Oh, sweetheart, this you just enjoy. Be grateful you didn't just get plunged into the womb of a new mother straight away. Here we relax, we enjoy the simple things we'll miss, like tasting cake and tea." She laughs here to keep things light. "And then we get dropped off to our next life and do it all over again." Dahlia thinks of something she misses tasting, something to help her relax, and if she could smoke it now or inject it into her veins while John folds her up and holds her in his arms then she would; this would be all she needs to get through. The absence of those arms suddenly leaves Dahlia feeling sick and frightened. "Your name was Emily and I was Cecilia and we were as thick as thieves, the two of us." She turns to her other friend opposite, who makes all the right faces and sounds of wonder and astonishment to encourage her.

"How do you remember me and I don't remember you?" Dahlia manages to ask, and she is not sure that she wants the answer. She wants her bed, she wants her drugs, and she wants her Johnnie.

"Have you not been to the Records?" There does seem to be a small detail in this woman's eyes that Dahlia thinks is familiar. But this something, this little bright sparkle, could be likened to many other encounters. Like the nice woman who walked Dahlia back to her mother when she got lost in the park, or the old man who let her choose a book for free in his second-hand store, or the only memory of her cousin Jackie, who was old enough to be Dahlia's aunt, bending down and looking into Dahlia's four-year-old eyes and telling her she was going to be a heartbreaker someday.

"What are the Records?" Dahlia looks at the two women, who are both delighted to enlighten her.

"Come with me," says the one who claims to know her. She stands up and takes Dahlia's hand, startling her. This touch is an odd sensation between two ghosts: it is a snap of electricity, like two raw wires connecting. But Dahlia doesn't take her hand away; she follows the woman through the next three carriages. "Sorry, I didn't tell you my name as it is now – it's Jane." Jane seems to have died when she was in her late twenties; there is youth in her presence, even in death. She wears a knee-length A-line denim skirt and a pale blue shirt, and her mousy-brown hair is brushed into a neat, low pony-tail that curls at the end. Dahlia guesses that she is from the mid-sixties, a time Dahlia remembers as her turbulent teenage years. Before they step into the next carriage, Jane takes a deep enthusiastic breath in as if to indicate that Dahlia must brace herself for what is beyond the door. Dahlia smiles at her for the first time, and Jane pulls her into the carriage.

If the ringmaster of a travelling circus possessed a library, this would be it. The interior is decorated in various tones of red and gold, glittered stars hang from the ceiling, and a scarlet velour chaise longue rests along one side of the carriage under the window. Wine-coloured velvet curtains are held back and tied with gold rope. Dark wood bookcases line the walls in an L-shape, and are filled to capacity with cloth-bound books of different colours. There is also a small round table, which is dressed in a diagonally striped red and gold cloth. Dahlia imagines that, much like a standard library, this is set up for comfortable and lengthy reading.

"What's your current name?" Jane asks, waiting for Dahlia's attention to come back to her.

"Dahlia Gregory," she mumbles, still taking in the vast number of books, the sparkles and all the different textures of this wonderful carriage.

"That's a beautiful name," Jane says as she bends down to get a better look at the names on the books, which have been alphabetised. She runs her fingers along the spines of the files like a child might down a staircase banister, making her fingers into little legs that skip with glee. "Dahlia Gregory, Dahlia Gregory. . ." she says until she finds it.

Jane hands Dahlia the file and there it all is on the front

blue cover embossed in silver: her date of birth, her date of death, and number of previous lives.

"I've had five lives?"

Jane nods as if she knew this. "When you open the book and go through them, it'll trigger all those memories. I should be in there somewhere. You'll see. We had a wonderful time together, you and I."

Just then Dahlia feels the train slowing down. "Are we stopping?" she asks, walking over to the window to look out. The flat open plains suddenly turn into stone walls and the light inside the carriage dims. "Are we stopping?" she asks again, urging Jane to confirm it. Dahlia now thinks of more passengers getting on and that possibly John could be one of them. She starts for the carriage door with her life file tucked under her arm and as she steps over into the next carriage, the train stops, screaming and cranking as it does so. Dahlia holds on to the back of an empty seat and when she regains her steady footing, she hurriedly makes her way back to her own carriage. She stops when she notices what's outside. The train has stopped just beside the mouth of a bridge that leads to a castle. The trees around it on the hillsides are dense and dark green – thick, wild forests. The sky is a chalky blue-grey. Whatever place this is, the clouds are keeping it contained, suffocating it almost.

Jane catches up with her and stands beside her to look out of the window. "Wow," she breathes, those watery blue eyes sparkling more than before. There are clusters of people walking towards the doors, some look sad, some look confused, and some look somewhat pleased and curious as if they are trying to get a good view of a street performer they are enjoying the sound of. None of them are John. But Dahlia thinks that there is still time for him to board. Maybe he will emerge from the back of the queue forming in front of the train. Dahlia carries on through the carriages back to her seat and the doors open to let the new souls on.

The woman from the fifties who was sitting near Dahlia is gone, and in her place is a young man of roughly Dahlia's age with soft, short, curly hair and green eyes. "Caroline has gone to her next life," the army officer leans over in his seat to explain to Dahlia.

"Oh." Dahlia is still trying to adjust to everything.

"Oh good, you have your life file, you must go through that," he says, nodding to the blue book that she still has clamped under her arm. She takes her seat and Erik begins his trolley round again from the back. The train has pulled away from the castle and is steaming through the thick forest greens. Everyone is seated and John has not come to join her. Jane must have gone back to her friend in the next carriage.

"It's hard, isn't it? When you're so young," the young man next to her says. The reflection of the trees whirring by outside rush across his eyes, like there is a reel of film playing across them.

"I didn't have much of a future anyway," Dahlia says in a mutter, her gaze now fixed on the front cover of her life file.

"What's that?" he asks, motioning to the book on her lap.

"It's a record of all my lives; I'm supposed to go through it. You need to go and retrieve yours in the Records carriage. Someone will show you." She feels that she could have been kinder, that perhaps she could make a friend while she waits, but she is feeling disappointed and subdued and wishes to be left alone, if only just while she reminisces.

"I'm Paul, by the way," he continues.

She acknowledges him gently. "I'm Dahlia." Paul gets the message that she wishes to be left awhile, and he gets up and walks through the carriage door to the next one.

She turns to the first page:

> Name: Katherine Heeley
> Nationality: British
> Date of Birth: August 19. 1422
> Date of Death: October 22. 1434
> Cause of Death: Starvation

The last word pulls at her gut. Just twelve years old, Dahlia thinks to herself. Upon the blank pages thereafter, images seem to appear like negatives being developed in a photo lab. A small skinny girl sits with her knees bent up against her chest. Just a crack of light shines on her filthy and tear-streaked face, which she rests to one side on her knees. Yes, Dahlia remembers now, she was locked in a closet by her father and was left to go hungry. The world was crueller back then compared to the mass desire of peace and harmony of the time she has just left, even though a war was still fought and cultures were still oppressed. But the darkness of the 1400s was a demon that would never let anyone rest. While she was dying, her waif of a body was hurting for a love that the world had whispered about but had never shown her. Katherine never saw it and so eventually, she no longer believed in it.

Again, Dahlia feels tears that cannot fall; they swell in her throat. She looks up from the book and into the blurry blues and greys of emptiness outside. The trees have gone and the train feels as though it has taken flight up into the sky, for there is nothing out there that watches them go by. Dahlia is reminded of her best friend, Joni, whom she met at summer camp in Idaho. They were both just twelve years old then. Joni carved Dahlia's name into a tree and she shared with Dahlia her allotted candy that her parents had sent her in the mail. Dahlia had been transferred into the custody of her uncle Larry after her parents died. Larry never sent her so much as a letter while Dahlia was at camp. Joni and Dahlia traded clothes and wrote each other secret notes and left them under each other's pillows in their bunk beds. When camp was over, Dahlia had locked Joni in her arms and couldn't let go, her tears soaking Joni's shoulder. They promised to write to each other, and they did, incessantly. For five solid years, Joni was the best thing in Dahlia's life, but then Joni decided she would study to be a translator in an international school in Germany. She became busy and stopped writing. Joni disappeared.

Dahlia pushes on through the book, remembering that in the late 1600s she was an Irish woman named Bronwyn who gave birth to a limp, blue baby. She screamed until her chest hurt and cursed the world and told it to never make her pregnant again. Dahlia remembers this depression, the catatonic states while lying on the bed, the tears that turned to stone on her cheeks, the words that wouldn't help her reach her husband. The death was long, and it was slow, but it was gratefully received when it came.

And then there was Jane as Cecilia and she as Emily, together always while their businessmen husbands travelled the world on boats and promises. They'd wile away their days on lazy walks around their gardens, playing a game of cards when the quiet nights could offer them a bottle of rum and each other's company. They'd have their houses redecorated, they'd chatter about clothes and libraries made and built for their future children. Emily had friendship, but she didn't have love. She had wealth, but no fulfilment. She doesn't remember the touch of her husband; she can feel his absence throughout this entire lifetime. She had died alone, old and bored. She remembers now her guide Leonie waiting for her after, and now she remembers Leonie asking for the same thing: belief. And yet Dahlia still hadn't acquired it. She begged for a life unlike the stiff, forced happiness she'd exhausted herself with in the Victorian era. Emily had wanted to explore, be thrown into excitement, shown passion, and be utterly moved by sheer experience. Leonie accepted her request and after a journey similar to this one, she stepped off the train, into the ball of white light, and on the other side had entered the womb of her new mother, who would name her first-born son Jacob. Jacob was to find himself on the borders of Munich in 1943: he would suffer violent shocks to his soul. He'd weep over small damaged bodies, he'd wear his toes down raw and bloody in heavy, garrotting boots, he'd curse the gun that he absolutely had to carry, his frightened hands greasing it with sweat. And then Jacob would decide that he had seen enough and couldn't be there anymore. He went AWOL and still the fear didn't leave him as he ran in the direction of home. He was found and, very swiftly, was killed. "Had you believed, Jacob, had you believed you would come home alive, you would have. You would have healed and you would have loved. But you took an early exit. You know that you must go back again," his guide had said.

Dahlia looks over at the officer again and he meets her eyes. This time there is something known between them, something she couldn't understand about his demeanour before. She does now. They have shared the same kind of hurt and have witnessed too much tragedy. He nods as if he has heard her thoughts; he understands. He takes a box of chocolates he has been resting on his lap and holds it out to her. "Would you like some? I couldn't eat them all, and Erik will be round again with more treats soon, I'm sure." He speaks to her with an American accent and this soothes her even more, for he is her kin. She takes the box, not because she would like a chocolate but because she wants to accept his kindness.

"Thank you," she replies and takes one, a salted caramel. It isn't a cigarette, a drink, or some junk, but it does taste like a little piece of happiness. "When will we be stopping again?" she asks him.

"Oh, probably not for another two months," he replies.

"Two months?" Dahlia panics – she cannot stand this train for that long.

"Well, you've been on this train for about two months already, dear," the woman in the silk blue gown says to her, joining the conversation. Neither the old man with the white fluffy hair nor the Native American woman look at them or chime in.

"How can that be possible? I've been here for what, an hour?" Dahlia asks.

"In earth time, yes. On this plane of existence, it is very different. I've been here for centuries, but it has felt like no time at all," she explains. Dahlia looks at the officer for confirmation.

"It's true."

Now Dahlia realises that John has been living without her for two months. She tries to imagine what he has been doing. Has he kept the apartment? Does he crawl onto their mattress and pick at the wallpaper on the wall above his head as he always did, and think of her as he does it? Does he crawl onto the mattress with someone else? She thinks of him out there still getting high with Eddie, or Savannah, or Michael; the thought of them all sinking into that liquid sunshine without her is like taking a punch to the stomach. If Earth is two months into the future, then it has ticked over from November to another year. It is 1972. How did John spend his New Year's Eve? Did he celebrate?

Dahlia turns back to the book and swiftly shuts it when the images of her mother in hospital begin to appear. Paul returns with his life file in his hand and takes a deep breath before he opens it. She finds her empathy for him and watches as he takes it all in. The train begins to slow down and the officer stands up. "It's time for me to go," he says to no one in particular. Dahlia looks at him sadly and then she turns to the window; there is a harbour coming into view. The water is still but is glistening. Sunshine has broken through.

"Where are you going?" Dahlia turns back to him.

"Japan, I am told. I'll be a humble fisherman." He laughs at this, straightening his uniform jacket again.

"How do you know that?" Paul asks, looking up from his book.

"My guide told me. I had a meeting with him this morning in carriage F. When you're ready, they call you and tell you where you're getting off." He takes one last gulp of his cup of tea and says, "I won't be able to drink this for a while." And as the train pulls in, he waves a goodbye to all the passengers and starts for the door.

"Wait!" Dahlia calls to him and stands up, holding onto the headrest of her seat. The officer stops and turns back to her. "What are you supposed to bring back?" she asks him.

He smiles affectionately at Dahlia before he answers. "Humility," he says, and the train then crunches as it stops in front of a pier, and soon the officer is gone.

No souls board the train at this stop. Dahlia tries to calm her anxious heart that still waits for her Johnnie to join her; she is starting to think he will not come. It feels like days before the scenery outside begins to change from the harbour to a green mountainous land, but in fact it is only a few hours. Dahlia thinks the landscape looks like Scotland. She'd thought that one day she might travel, but John never wanted to leave his apartment, let alone America. She has seen more riding this train than she ever did while she was living on Earth.

A total of forty-two hours have passed since Dahlia boarded this train and back in Earth-reality, years have gone by. Neither Dahlia nor any of the other passengers have slept; the dead do not need to. She has passed her time going through her book again and eating treats from Erik's trolley, and she has opened up to Paul, who, after remembering that he had once killed someone in self-defence in 1940s' New York, was severely distressed. If he could cry, his face would've been soaked. He'd paced up and down the train, clutching at his hair. He was trying to shake off the image of the light in the man's eyes extinguishing at the puncture Paul's knife had made. Dahlia tries to believe that after Paul's eight tragic previous lives, surely it means he will be rewarded with a simple and happy one next. It would be too cruel otherwise. He'd seen murder, committed murder, been raped, been robbed, been beaten, and in each life he'd never made it past the age of thirty-five.

"I can't keep doing this. I want it to be over, I want there to be nothingness," Paul says. Dahlia has followed him to carriage E where he rests against the door and rubs his temples. There is no physical headache but the pain is there.

"I know, I feel like I'm going crazy here," she replies. "But here's the thing: I thought I was going crazy back there too, and at least on this train, in between, I get to take a break from having to be me. To wake up every morning and try to find a job, be rejected, receive bills through the mail, and prove to people that I will do well someday."

Paul nods along in agreement. "But isn't it hell to know what we know now, to know that we have to do this all over again?" he questions.

Dahlia completely understands, but she also wants to appease his suffering. But it is difficult trying to do that and quieten down her own suffering at the same time. "We do this again until we've learned what we're supposed to learn and bring back what we're supposed to bring back." She feels herself channelling Leonie's guidance in this moment.

"What are you supposed to bring back with you?" Paul asks her.

"Belief," she replies, and that simple word seems silly for her to use. She laughs a little and this makes him smile. "And you?" she asks.

He rubs a hand through his hair again, a nervous habit he seems to permanently possess. "Peace," he replies quietly, and quickly follows it with, "it's not an easy one."

An hour later, the train pulls into a platform in a desert. She thinks of Arizona and the time she and John drove through it to see his sister in Colorado. She thinks of those fresh mountains now. She would give anything to feel that clean again. It makes her wish that she was back there, holding hands with John, the two of them breathing deep into their lungs as they let the sunshine stream across their faces. They were happy that weekend, they were sober, and their love for each other was heightened by the purity of that mountain air and the clarity of their senses. Everything felt fresh to Dahlia, including her soul. But all she sees is desert now, rough yellows and parched, cracked land, and her mouth feels suddenly dry. She takes a cup of ginger and lemon tea from Erik's trolley, a drink John's sister had introduced her to on their visit. She takes one back for Paul. They wait for the newly-dead to board the train, and the ones about to be newly-born leave. Jane is one of them. She gives Dahlia a hearty goodbye and is gone with as much enthusiasm as she had managed to sustain throughout the entire journey. There is still no John, but there is Paul, and Dahlia feels they are forging a friendship; there is an understanding between them.

"I was thinking, about peace, and what it means to have it." She begins this conversation with Paul, who is slumped up against the window, cradling his cup of tea with both hands. He drags his eyes away from the scenery outside to meet hers. "I thought I'd found peace," she continues, "in love and in drugs."

"Isn't there peace in love, though? If it's the right kind of love?" Paul responds. His voice comes out raspy and dry.

She nods in agreement. "Yes, that's true. The right kind of love is worth everything. But I was taking drugs to numb everything else. Loving my boyfriend was the only thing I could manage." She wants to tell him about it all, she wants to talk about her parents dying, about being alone, about finding John, and the other ways she escaped reality. And she wants to tell him that after everything Paul had been through, her last life seemed actually quite kind. She was at least given the chance to be lucky; Paul was never given the same choices.

"Was it the drugs that killed you?" Paul asks her after reflecting on the lack of love in his lives. Dahlia bows her head and looks into her teacup.

"Yes, and I didn't care. That's the most stupid thing about it, I didn't care." Dahlia hands Paul her book, but he doesn't take it straight away. "Just go through it. You'll understand exactly what I'm feeling now."

Erik approaches them from down the aisle, this time without a trolley but instead a small card in his hand. "Dahlia Gregory, this is for you." Erik gives it to her and swiftly turns on his heel and heads back the way he came. All eyes are on her.

"I think you're being summoned," says the woman in the silk gown.

Dahlia opens the note. It reads: "Please report immediately to carriage F." Dahlia sets her cup down on the table rest, gives Paul a warm gaze and then rises from her seat, "I have to go."

In carriage F, Leonie is waiting for her. Dahlia is surprised to see her again and also surprised to find that the carriage is bare and void of any colour, decor, curtains, or any other embellishments like those of the Records carriage. There are no windows in this carriage either, only two simple chairs, one for the soul and one for the guide. "Please sit." Leonie's warm voice is a comfort to hear again, but seeing her here means that it is time for Dahlia to move on, and this makes her nervous. "You've been in the afterlife for some Earth years now, although here it may have only seemed like a short time," Leonie says, looking right into Dahlia's eyes. "But I think you're ready." She locks her fingers and rests her hands on her lap like someone in a meditation pose.

"I don't know if I am ready," Dahlia replies. She knows Leonie can feel whatever she is feeling, as guides are empaths after all.

"You will alight at the next stop. You're heading to rural Ireland for a life of devoting yourself to the church."

Dahlia wants to know details. Does that mean she won't have sex? She'll never take drugs? Never party or fall in love? After Leonie has heard her thoughts, her face shifts into an expression of something between sympathy and concern. "But what is it about these things that you enjoyed and will miss? They're all pleasurable, aren't they," Leonie says. Dahlia nods in agreement. "Well, you will be in love with something entirely different; you will enjoy other pleasures. You must remember, Dahlia, you won't be who you are now."

Dahlia returns to her carriage. Paul looks up from her life file, which he has been reading, and smiles at her until he realises that her expression is serious and contemplative. "When do you go?" he asks.

"The next stop." She holds her hand out to indicate that she needs her file back, "I have to return it to the Records." Paul, almost not wanting to let it go, passes it to her slowly.

"I understand now," he says, looking directly into her eyes, urging her to comprehend his sentiment. Dahlia smiles back gently and heads to the Records carriage to file her book of lives away.

Dahlia takes her final time on the Earth-bound Express to look out at the lakes and mountains they are passing. She realises just how serene it is to sit with nothing to do but recognise the beauty of the world, take in the colours, the textures, and the bounty. She is excited to step onto real ground again and feel space all around her. But first she will watch her mother and father smiling at her, feel the warmth of them as her incapable body is cradled against their chests. She will learn to talk and to put her feet on that ground as if for the first time; she will learn to do it all over again. She takes a slice of cheesecake and coffee knowing that she will soon forget what they are and how wonderful they taste. Erik wishes her good luck; Paul cannot say goodbye.

The train slows as it approaches its next stop. The year is 1980. She waves at her travel companions and bids an almost nostalgic farewell to death; it had been more kind to her than her living in those days of sixties' America. The train halts in front of a small farmhouse in a wet, dark-green field. The doors open and Dahlia's nerves rattle up again in her soul.

Only one passenger is waiting to board, and there he is; it is finally him.

"Dahlia," John whispers, his tired, aged face lifts with relief. Her beloved John finally came. After all these years, he followed. If he could cry, he would.

"Johnnie." She lifts a hand to touch his thin, lined skin. He is skinny, almost to the bone. His cheeks have sunken in; his teeth are askew and tinted with yellow stains. "I missed you so much," he says, but Dahlia isn't sure he missed her enough from what she sees in him now. The damage done to his body over decades of destruction and greed suggest he hadn't. The train blows its horn to signal its departure.

Dahlia steps down onto the field next to him and says, "Another time." She watches his guide, a tall and broad gentleman in a bowler hat and suit, who nudges John forwards onto the train. The doors close and John's face doesn't turn away from Dahlia until the train moves on and the carriage is out of sight. Behind her is the entrance to the tunnel of white light, where all will be erased to make way for the new. The only thing she must remember is to believe.

Dark Arts and Deities

DRIVEN TO FAUSTIAN despair, a woman named Carla made a deal with some gods one night and brought an entire town down to its knees. She called out to whatever was out there and her cries were most certainly heard. She'd read about blues musicians making deals with demons at crossroads, she'd heard of people working with voodoo to get what they wanted, but Carla got something very unique indeed. One wet and blustery night during the time where autumn climbs into its colder, thicker skin of winter, Greek, Roman, Hindu, Japanese and other great entities of long ago came down to Earth to meet her.

Carla had been making quite a reputation for herself in the town of Red Oak, where she had moved to two months before, to get away from the ruined past she'd left back in her home city.

Red Oak was a pretty little town with a tight community. So proud of its resplendent front gardens and its picturesque town square and clock tower, its abundance of high quality pie bakers and smart, polite children. None of it had been prepared for the arrival of Carla and her drive for doing whatever she wanted with whomsoever she wanted. Red Oak liked order, and it had trembled when it felt that chaos stepping off a train and walking through the square in a long black dress and a crown of dark curls that would have made Medusa proud.

Carol Abbott, the local pharmacist, shouldn't have tutted and whispered when Carla blew past. Carla had heard the unfavourable comments about her appearance and noted them in her mind for later – Carol would get what she deserved for that.

Carla moved into a small cottage that was probably the ugliest house in the whole town, but it was still decent enough to keep its kerb-appeal reputation afloat. She immediately set about finding herself a job. Ruth Simmons told Carla that there were no vacancies at the town's favourite restaurant. Sally Hodgkin said no without letting Carla finish her enquiry at the dry-cleaner's, and old Cyril Dodd gawped at her for quite some time at the grocer's before he could paste together an answer, which was that he wasn't sure, well maybe, possibly not. Carla gave up for the day and went back to her empty cottage to cry. No one had ever seen Carla cry, not even her own mother. What most people feared about Carla was that she always appeared cold and void of emotion. But even as a naughty child, when she was stealing dolls and siding with villains, she was just as sensitive as anyone. She'd believed that there was a great injustice in the world and that's what had led her to her selfish acts.

There had always been something different about Carla, even when she was a young girl. Her mother had thought that there was some kind of darkness in Carla. It began small, with her stealing a toy she wanted from Victoria's eighth birthday party because she'd been eyeing up that doll in the shops for quite a long time. She once stuck out her foot and tripped Jason up on the assembly hall steps at school because he'd said that her hair smelled of egg sandwiches.

Then it grew into less minor incidents. Carla had seduced a colleague at work, just to spite his long-time admirer, Janet, who'd been saying nasty things about Carla around the office. Carla had for some reason taught herself to satisfy her appetites, and if others were hurt in the process, then so be it.

When Carla was eight years old, she took an interest in witchcraft, and her mother, Elaina, had voiced her concerns to Carla's father. He had responded by saying, "Children are fascinated by the idea of magic. She'll grow out of it." Elaina had dropped the subject for a while, but was still unnerved when Carla cackled in front of the TV when villains did evil deeds in cartoons – and even more so when Carla set up her toys into a horror scene in her bedroom.

"Mister Bear was stabbed in the heart for telling lies about Polly," Carla had explained, with red paint on her fingers. "Mister Bear's blood," she added casually to her mother, who remained silent on the edge of the bed.

Carla had also always wanted to dress up as a powerful sorcerer on Halloween. "What a delightful imagination!" Victoria's mother had once said, unaware of what happened to the doll cousin Alison had bought for Victoria – she assumed the dog had got to it. Alfie often enjoyed burying miscellaneous items in the backyard.

It was when Carla's grandfather Clarence passed away that death and dark feelings became real for Carla. Carla was eleven years old by then and had stopped playing with Mister Bear and Polly the Doll. Following her grandfather's death, she chose not to speak for two years, taking a vow of silence, which made things difficult for her parents and her teachers.

Carla would only write down the words she wished to communicate. She had also taken to finding occult books in the library and brought them home to read, much to her mother's alarm. Until Grandfather Clarence died, everything to Carla had seemed timeless; eternity had been given to her to play with. She could do wrong and right, and twist and turn as she pleased, because life, to her, was endless. She could start over if things didn't go her way.

Elaina eventually took Carla to a child therapist. The therapist had brought up the subject of power struggles within the parenthood dynamic. After two sessions, Elaina stopped taking Carla to therapy. "Please speak, darling," she'd said to the girl statue sitting next to her in the passenger seat of the car. Carla was watching an old man get into the car in front of them with the help of a younger man, who must have been his son. *Death is coming for you soon*, Carla had thought with sadness.

"You like stories, don't you, Carla? About magic? Well, do you know any stories about gods?" Elaina had asked, desperate to engage with her daughter. Carla's eyes fell to her mother's hands on the steering wheel. "Well there were these Greek gods, one was called Zeus and one was called Poseidon and Poseidon ruled the seas . . ." Elaina told Carla all about the gods who played with weather.

Carla finally asked, "And where are they now, Mummy?"

Elaina's tears fell freely at the sound of her daughter's voice, which she hadn't heard in two years. "I don't know, my angel. They're out there somewhere. Look at the sun breaking through," she said, pointing to the sky. "That must be Apollo making it shine." And so Carla stopped taking books about witches out from the library and started to bring home ones about mythology instead.

If there was anything that did soften her over the years, it was a boy named Ocean, whose eyes looked like rain clouds. And if you looked deep into those heavy grey eyes, you could almost see the clouds shifting and drifting, like the brewing of a storm. With Ocean's name so great, and his eyes so brooding, his face in contrast was pearly and soft, and his heart was even more so.

Ocean and Carla met at university in a Classical Civilisation class. Ocean was often distracted in class by Carla's dark brown eyes, and her mahogany curls. They partnered up for a class project and went to the museum together to look at the Greek statues. And over coffee afterwards, Carla let Ocean speak about his interests in folklore and that perhaps he'd want to teach it or write about it someday. She loaded up questions in her mind as he spoke; she wanted to know everything about him all at once. She wanted to know how he had got his name and what his parents were like. She wanted to know if he had felt different to all the other kids too when he was growing up. She wanted to know why he had taken an interest in her.

Carla had been shy with Ocean, which she found herself surprised by - she had never been shy in her life. She noticed herself being composed and almost meek. Later that afternoon with Ocean, after the museum and the coffee shop, the two of them went for a walk along the river. They shared a cinnamon bun and sidled up close. When the winds kicked up, Carla felt like she was about to jump into a tornado. Ocean's eyes, his warmth, and the rumbling waters, prompted her to ask him:

"Ocean, if I were a mythical creature, what would I be?"

"You'd be a goddess," he'd replied, looking up to the sky. Then he brought his eyes down to meet hers, and leant in for a kiss. The tornado passed and left her standing there in the calm.

Carla had everything she needed as long as she had Ocean. She didn't need to steal what she didn't have, nor punish anyone for their lies and trouble. None of this mattered except the ever-growing fear of losing him. She finally understood that having what she wanted wasn't as important as losing what she already had. She started to live life carefully.

A year later, after thousands of kisses, soft smiles, strokes along torsos and hot breath in the crook of the neck, Ocean left Carla's life just as swiftly as he had entered it. Transferred to Boston because of his father's work, Ocean promised to phone and write. And as soon as Carla could afford a plane ticket, they'd be together again. But there was something about Carla that Ocean's mother had never liked and had never admitted. Thinking that Carla wasn't good enough for her son, and hearing from other mothers that Carla had always suffered with mental issues, she intervened and cut the ties between Carla and Ocean. She blocked the house telephone from connecting long-distance calls and made sure that Ocean's new American mobile phone couldn't take them either. When he had disputed it, his mother just kicked up a fuss about the costs. Ocean and Carla had never even exchanged email addresses; they'd thought it would be more romantic to just keep it at letters and calls. Ocean's mother had offered to post Ocean's letters for him, and any that were addressed to Carla were thrown into the rubbish bin, streets away from the house. Whenever Carla dialled the number Ocean had given her, she'd hear the telephone woman telling her repeatedly that her call could not be connected. And envelopes arriving to their house in Boston from Carla were quickly torn and tossed into street bins as well. Ocean's mother simply thought that one or the other's feelings would fade eventually. After all, they were very young.

After a year of no phone calls and unanswered letters, Carla began to burn with anger instead of love. She was hurting badly. She lost all faith in everyone. After graduating from university, Carla had managed to find herself a job working as an office junior for a mediocre company in the city. Her grief over Ocean soon became mixed up with recklessness, and she began causing trouble among her colleagues. The women ostracised her and didn't hide the fact, either. Carla flirted with the men and slept with a few, even some who were married. She didn't care because she had nothing to care about anymore.

And while she was raising hell, she would never know that a heartbroken Ocean was sending her tender thoughts, still believing that he'd get her back someday. Burning too many bridges around her, Carla finally snapped and decided that she wanted to leave everything and make a new start somewhere else. Carla left her job, left the city and her home, and never saw her parents again.

And so now, at the age of twenty-three, she was living in a town she had never been to before. She needed a job and was running out of options. She was finding it tedious; she was receiving the same sort of reaction from the people in Red Oak as she had in her office back in the city. But this time, she had done nothing to lead them to believe that she was trouble. They just simply didn't like the look of her.

While sipping a cappuccino at Kathy's, the town's only coffee shop, Carla got into a conversation with Peter Biggins, a local contractor, who was too curious about Carla to not speak to her. Peter asked Carla what had brought her to Red Oak and she told him that it was a fresh start and nothing more. She said that she was trying to get a job but no one seemed to be hiring, and Peter asked her what area of work she was qualified for, to which Carla replied, "Classical civilisation." Peter wasn't entirely sure what that was, but guessed that it had something to do with old things, and so he suggested that she see Nicholas Beasley, the owner of the antique shop, about a position. Carla told Peter that it wasn't quite the same thing but it was close enough, and she thanked him for his help. Peter swirled his cup of milky tea and then backed it. He then said that he thought she seemed rather young to be into old things and history. Carla simply replied, "I'm an old soul."

Nicholas felt slightly out of his depth talking to a bright, young, attractive woman about the Greek rhetoric of power and how female presence was lacking in her chosen field. But not wanting to come across sexist or uneducated, he hired her. He wasn't sure what Carla's title would be, but he showed her the books, gave her a list of phone numbers alongside a list of artefacts, and asked her to give those people a call to tell them that their items of interest were in. Carla quickly grew bored, and to pass the time she'd eye Mr Beasley up and picture him naked, not because she found him attractive but because it was a fun mental game. Carla's sexual appetite had always been that of a nymph's, and without uni boys and promising colleagues to prey on, she was left with slim pickings.

After weeks of working at the antiques shop and drinking away her lonely hours in the Red Oak pub, Christmas was looming, and all was jolly and light. Feeling sorry for Carla, who had no one to share the festivities with, Nicholas invited her over for Christmas dinner. He'd mentioned his wife, Beth, to Carla before, but had never mentioned that he had an eighteen-year-old son named Lawrence. It only took a week for Lawrence to come back to her after they'd slept together, begging at her door for more tantric fornication.

Lawrence had his own admirer by the name of Rachel Abbott, the daughter of Carla's greatest slanderer, Carol. Mother and daughter worked together in the bar at the Red Oak and Rachel had started spitting in Carla's whisky when she wasn't looking. Carla would drink down her liquid warmth with relish, and would laugh along with Beth, who also enjoyed a drink. Beth had no clue that her son was having sex with her drinking partner on a frequent basis. A regular named Ernest Baxter had seen Rachel gobbing into the glasses of Jameson and told Carla what was happening in a whisper on his way out of the door. Carla had launched a few invisible arrows with her eyes across the bar but didn't tell Beth what she had just been told. Ernest, the retired furniture upholsterer, thought he was doing good by letting Carla know. He also told Owen Reeves, Rachel's college tutor. Ernest thought that perhaps Rachel's character could be straightened out during class hours if it couldn't be under the supervision of her mother. Ernest's divulging however went on to do more harm.

Owen, a thirty-two-year-old Media Studies tutor, had been working on his student in his own way. Rachel didn't pay enough attention in class, and she also didn't pay attention to where her stretch miniskirt ended up by the end of the lesson as she squirmed in her seat and dug into her pockets to check messages on her phone. Owen did pay attention, and to him, four years of no sex warranted the seizing of an opportunity with a not-so-bright-but-legal girl who could show him the talents she possessed outside the arena of study. When Owen asked Ernest what Rachel's motives were for doing such a crass thing to the new girl in town, Ernest had only suggested that something Carla had done had clearly riled her. Owen knew who Lawrence Beasley was, and had come to the right conclusions when he noticed Rachel in the hall with him on a few occasions, chatting with him flirtatiously. Owen didn't like that. He started to keep a close eye on the boy Rachel took a particular interest in.

Some weeks down the line, Owen decided to knock Lawrence – who he thought to be a cocky little peacock – off his cloud. Having a narcissistic boy around was never good for any man. On a night that started off in the Red Oak, Owen befriended Lawrence and got him well and truly paralytic. The night ended with Lawrence shivering violently in a blackened field some eight miles outside of town. Owen was no murderer, but thought a lesson in greater fears would be good for Lawrence's modesty. And if Lawrence wanted to be a man that banged girls like Rachel and, as he later found out through alcohol-lubricated honesty, Carla as well, then maybe a cold, lonely night in the middle of nothingness might make him realise his true place. Lawrence phoned Carla the next afternoon after some eventual sleep against the trunk of a tree and a sore, snail-paced walk home. He had told her about his drinks with Owen and his terror out in the dark, but had completely drawn a blank on everything in between. Carla had never loved anyone but her dearest Ocean – and never would again – but she was fond of Lawrence. And like a true calculated master of vengeance, with the need to take karmic matters into consideration, she knew that some chain of events had led to Lawrence being shafted by Owen and her drink being spat in. While Carla was working out how best to deal with the likes of Owen and Rachael, her boss, Nicholas, paid her a visit on his day off.

Nicholas's voice had been more curt than usual and he didn't bring his eye up from her doormat until he'd said that matters were delicate and he needed to speak with her. Carla invited him into the living room, where he didn't take off his coat and took some time deliberating on whether to sit on the sofa or the tattered and pilled armchair. He chose the armchair. He didn't want to be sitting too close to Carla in case she got angry after what he had to tell her.

"Now, I'm afraid you've put me in quite a position, Carla," Nicholas began. Carla then interjected with the offer of tea. Nicholas quickly shook his head as if her interruption would make him forget his lines. "I know about you and Lawrence. And quite frankly, Beth and I both agree that the situation is quite distasteful." Carla opened her mouth to speak and Nicholas insisted that she let him finish. "Now, you're very handy to have at the shop, I'll admit, and I was growing quite fond of having you there. But now Rachel has expressed some business that has been rather hurtful to her, and in turn to

Carol, who I believe is a couple of moves away from coming down here to visit you. And I think you'll agree that you won't want that sort of mess on your doorstep." Carla's lips had tightened at the mention of Rachel and Carol. "Carla, I'm not sure if where you come from people would deal with certain matters in the way we deal with things here. People in Red Oak certainly do not like to play crude games." Carla put her hand up to Nicholas indicating to him quite firmly that here she would interrupt.

"A game such as the one Rachel plays with my drinks at the pub? Have you heard about that one, Nicholas?" Nicholas cleared his throat and went on to wave that part of the story away.

"Beth and I were beside ourselves the night Lawrence didn't come home. And that's not like our boy, to be so inebriated that he'd spend the night shivering in the middle of God knows where. There's a conversation to be had with Owen Reeves, but that's beside the point. Lawrence is eighteen, and you're what, twenty-three? Something like that?" Carla nodded in response. She straightened her body, raising herself up like the cobra she could be. "Well, that's just not on," Nicholas continued. "He's vulnerable and I dare say that we didn't have drama in this town before you came along." Carla told him to get to the point. "Very well, you're not to see Lawrence again – Beth's wishes ultimately. And you will not work for me any longer."

Carla thought of many things she could tell Nicholas, but she held them in. The cobra wouldn't bite this time; she'd save it for the person who really deserved the attack. But Carla thought she'd leave him with a few things to think about.

"I'm very disappointed in you, Nicholas. If you think that I'm the problem in Red Oak then I suggest you dig out those glasses you keep on a shelf in the shop instead of on your face and take a look around. I presume you've told Lawrence we aren't to see each other again?" Nicholas fiddled with the button on his coat and told her that Beth had spoken to him and there was no more to it. "May I just say, Nicholas, that if you're so concerned with Rachel being upset – and I also presume you've known Carol for a long time – then perhaps you ought to ask Owen, when you have that chat, why Rachel's well-being is so important to him. Why is it so important that he'd feel the need to teach Lawrence a lesson for hurting her feelings? Surely a college tutor wouldn't care that much about the private affairs of one of his female students, would he?" And Carla left that hanging in the air as she rose to her feet to show Nicholas out the door. She waited a good second or two as Nicholas caught up to what was happening and rose to his feet also. "Thank you for the work you gave me. I thoroughly enjoyed being at the shop. All the best now, Nicholas." Carla slammed the door behind him and began to tremble.

A single tear ran down Carla's cheek before she smacked it away like the pest it was and clenched her fists. She thought about losing her job and about Nicholas who had been such a piece of wet cardboard under the influence of others. She thought about Owen and his perversions. She was angry with Carol and her bitchy tongue and Rachel and her pathetic excuse for an existence. And she was angry at Lawrence for not being Ocean. Carla screamed, not high and shrill like a banshee, but low and growling like an animal warning a predator off. Soon the veins in her arms were straining against the surface of her skin, her teeth were threatening to crumble from the tension she held there with her jaws. And before she knew it, she was chanting a conjuring spell she'd memorised when she was a young girl. "Gods, goddesses, I call to thee! Hear my cry and hear my plea! Gods, goddesses, banish the weakness in me. Mighty spirits, give me the power and strength I need!" Carla's voice vibrated in that small cottage, and when it stopped, a silence that was much louder than her calls blanketed the air. Carla let the tears escape and mock her as she fell to the floor with her fists balled, keeping at bay the desire to tear her own hair out.

With her cheeks numb and her eyelids heavy, Carla finally got up from the floor. The room was suddenly drowning in an Aegean blue; the day had turned to night. Carla decided on being spared a quiet night awake and instead dragged herself up the stairs to bed.

Perhaps it was the sudden downpour that was battering against the windows, the roof, and the ground outside that awoke Carla after only a few hours of sleeping. But perhaps Carla was responding to a sixth sense she didn't even know she possessed. Because waiting patiently on the end of Carla's bed was Athena, the Greek goddess of battle, twirling her spear, causing winks of white light to dart across the bedroom wall as Carla stirred. Carla first looked up at the window above her bed to confirm that there was, in fact, noisy and aggressive weather beating itself against her house. She then looked down to her feet where she could see, in the flashes of lightning, a woman with hair the colour of cinnamon bark and eyes perhaps blue or grey, which were looking back at her with expectation. Carla only became slightly frightened when she caught sight of the spear, along with the shield sitting on the floor, propped up against the base of the bed. "No, you're not dreaming, sweet child," Athena said, just to move things along. "And yes, I'm Athena. You called me down along with a few others as well. We're here now, so I don't suppose you could come downstairs and speak with us?"

"Pardon?" Carla's eyes were puffy from crying and tiredness, but she was certain of what was happening. She was partly scared that the conjuring had worked, but mostly, she was delighted. Now things could really begin for her.

Just as Athena had explained, there were a fair few companions gathered in the living room downstairs waiting for her. A god, not large but muscular, who stood by the fireplace caught Carla's eye first, because even though his skin was a grey-blue, his adornments were bright and opulent. Half his long brown hair was piled up on his head in a cone shape that was decorated with a gold band that matched his hooped earrings. A red, diamond, squiggle-shaped bindi sat between his eyebrows like a tiny pet snake, and his neck was weighed down by beads that seemed to have been wrapped around him countless times, like a mile-long scarf. He wore no clothes on his body other than a wrap of red and gold cloth around his waist, and next to him, resting against the mantelpiece, was a gleaming trident. Carla presumed he was Shiva. "Correct, Carla" He had heard her thoughts and responded with a twist in his accent that rang true to his Indian tongue. "See if you can guess the others," Shiva said to Carla, pulling one side of his lips into a smirk.

He looked down at a beautiful, long-limbed and sultry

blonde who was sitting diagonally across the sofa. One of her legs was crossed over the other, under her ankle-length and almost see-through white dress. The beauty smiled. She brought her shoulders up and turned her head, enjoying the spotlight for a moment. "Long, luscious blonde hair – an almost pagan appearance. British, perhaps? Are you Sulis?" Carla guessed.

"Freyja actually, and I'm Nordic. I thought you would have known that," Freyja answered. Carla could now hear the Nordic bend in her almost-perfect English accent. Freyja was the goddess of sexuality, beauty, and love, and Carla had always enjoyed reading about her provocations and seductions in the books she studied.

"Well, it's a pleasure," Carla said.

She stepped a little further into the room, slightly distracted by the sound of Athena's armour beside her. "Yoohoo, Carla! Over here, my darling." A short and slim but toned god waved at her from the armchair. Mercury gave himself away by his Roman eloquence and the winged helmet on his head. "I am known for my poetic heart and equally for my trickery. And goodness me, am I excited to know what tricks you wish me to perform tonight." A goddess with long, flat, and thin black hair told Mercury to settle down because no one had discussed the deal yet. Ribbons of red silk fluttered from her sleeves as she spoke. Her gown covered her toes. She stood rather centrally in the room, but against Shiva's gold and Freyja's glaring beauty, Carla had initially missed her. Carla knew she was Chinese, but wasn't familiar with the goddess herself. Chang'e rolled her eyes and announced herself.

"Goddess of the moon," she added in a tone that suggested

this was all rather tedious. A burst of thunder growled over-head, and although Carla knew it was pouring with rain outside, something told her that the god who stepped in from behind the stairs had casted it.

"You probably won't know me; your studies aren't as vast as you may think they are in the West. I'm Raijin. I'm Japanese, and as you've guessed, I'm god of thunder and lightning." This one excited Carla the most. Raijin had a beastly presence, a low gruff voice and canines that could rip into the jugular effortlessly. His thick black hair was puffed and crazed behind him. Most of all, his eyes were wide and manic, just like all the villains she had known and loved in her favourite cartoons as a child. And quite peculiarly, Raijin's ears were sharp at the tips, like an elf's. He was the greatest powerhouse in the room; Carla could feel it coming off him in waves, and it rattled her with wickedness and excitement. "So here we all are, Carla" Raijin continued. "You called us down. Tonight is your night."

Carla sat down by Freyja, who smelt of violets, wet leaves, and honey. Athena explained that the gods had been paying close attention to Carla ever since she was born. "You have always had a particular kind of strength and power, and we believe your soul can ascend into deity status." Carla raked the curls at the back of her head with her trimmed oxblood-painted fingernails and bounced her gaze from one divine being to another. She lost focus for a moment and was wondering if they ate or drank. Perhaps they'd enjoy some wine.

"Some wine would be beautiful, if you have any." Shiva had responded to her thoughts again. Mercury agreed enthusiastically that they should have some wine.

Just hours before, Carla had been sobbing her eyes out in

painful rage. Now she was socialising with the ancient beings she'd read about in books. All of her emotional cuts were quickly closing up now; this would be her healing. It was all surreal and amusing, and yet, to Carla, it was absolutely acceptable. She had always believed otherworldly entities to exist. She fetched the wine and noticed her fingers trembling as she lifted some glasses out of her cupboard. She felt nervous and giddy and special.

"Let's get straight to the point, Carla," Chang'e said as she shook her head at the offer of a glass of red when the tray came round to her. "We can teach this town a lesson for you, but of course, if your memory or study serves, we don't use our powers without something in return." Carla set the tray down on the coffee table, took a sip of her wine and reminded herself to sit up straight. Freyja gave her a wink and Shiva's adornments jangled a little as he shifted position. Carla didn't need to be smart to know that they would ask something great of her in return. She was prepared to give them what they wanted. But she had something she wanted even more than tearing Red Oak to pieces.

"You want your beloved Ocean, is that correct?" Shiva's eyes met Carla's. There was no blocking out her thoughts to his ears. And although this would be a liability, she was rather impressed. A tree branch outside smacked itself against the window. A flash of violent lightning threw streaks across Chang'e's smooth, marble-like face. Despite being angry with Ocean for not calling her or writing to her, Carla still missed him terribly and loved him more than ever. There must have been some other reason he didn't contact her; she had felt that he would always love her.

"I do want him. But I want to know what you want from me first." Carla reminded herself that she must remain confident in this moment. If Chang'e wanted to intimidate Carla, then she had met her match. Carla rose to her feet. "You want my soul? You can have it when I die. But I get Ocean back and we'll spend our lives together. Happily." Raijin raised a fuzzy black eyebrow and Mercury smiled at Carla and looked back to Chang'e, whose face went from challenging to pleased.

"Let's review, shall we?" Athena said, stepping towards Carla, sounding like a bag of chains as she moved, her breasts shifting weight between themselves behind her breastplate. "These people have done you wrong. More importantly, they are nasty pieces of work – to take an earthly expression." Freyja then chimed in to explain that they were fully aware of all the snaky movements of Carla's foes in Red Oak. And that, in fact, Carla didn't quite have the full picture.

Freyja explained that Rachel Abbott had found out that it was Ernest who had snitched on her to Carla and Owen Reeves for spitting into Carla's drinks. Rachel then went to pay him a visit. When he had refused to answer the door, Rachel began vandalising Ernest's front garden. She had snapped his pear trees and kicked pots up into the air. She tore at his hedges, and she had contemplated smashing the stained-glass panel on his front door – but even she knew that that would be going too far. "The little bitch," Carla said through gritted teeth. Shiva watched Carla's jaw twitch and was excited by the fanned flames. There was more to the little circuit of crude behaviour to come: Sally Hodgkin, Carol's best friend and the woman who had rebuffed Carla in the dry-cleaners when she was looking for work, had a secret that she was keeping nice and tight in her underwear.

The previous New Year's Eve, Carol was working in the bar, as she did every year, and her husband, who Carla was also elated to hear existed, was more than drunk and more than bored that evening. In Carol's absence, he had taken himself to a little soirée at Sally's, which ended with all but one of the guests leaving after midnight, to either continue drinking at the Red Oak or take themselves off home to bed. The guest who was left standing, Carol's husband, and host Sally ended up lying on the sofa. Hands went down trousers and tongues charged into Bacardi-soaked mouths. And Sally didn't leave that indiscretion where it was on that special occasion, but for some weeks afterwards took to riding Carol's husband in the couple's bed when Carol and Rachel were working the Friday-night shift at the pub. It had been Jeremy, Carol's hairy, short, and bony husband, who had broken the affair off. He's always regretted sleeping with Sally and took his secret with him to the grave.

"Now, Jeremy could come in quite handy for dealing with Owen Reeves, who hasn't just been looking up Rachel's skirt in class. The naughty college tutor has also recently been texting his student pictures of himself," Shiva piped up, now on to his second glass of wine.

"These pictures go slightly beyond an innocent image of how proud he is to be getting a six pack. They show everything but the tip of his cock," Mercury mused. "If Jeremy is like any other father of a teenage daughter, he'll obliterate Owen when he finds out."

Carla's mind was working alongside those of the gods and goddesses now, and saw how hitting all those vile people at once would be glorious and effortless. She desperately wanted to make an example of them. "Like little dominoes they'll go down – one by one," Raijin said, illustrating the action of a tsunami with his forefinger. "We'll set the scene," he continued, and demonstrated his point by casting another growl of thunder outside.

"You're aware of the moon myth aren't you, Carla?" Chang'e asked. "How the full moon turns people – sends them crazy, unleashes werewolves, et cetera?" Chang'e then put her arms straight out in front of her, palms facing outwards, as if she were pressing them against an invisible wall.

"Of course," Carla replied, the sparkle in her eyes dancing.

"Well, the tides are high tonight." Chang'e closed her eyes as if she were mentally communing with the moon itself. *Yes, make them go crazy!* Carla thought.

"I'll be paying Owen a visit," said Freyja, who stood up and took both her arms and bent them at the elbows and then crossed them before her face. She transformed herself into an ordinary girl – hair tied in a ponytail and her face softened with an innocence that wasn't there before. Freyja was now wearing a cream slip dress with buttons at the chest. Her breasts were pushed up a little, and she was wearing a pair of tights and a woolly cardigan for just a little bit of modesty. It was perfect for her role. "Do I fit in as a teenage girl with the body of someone who's wickedly experienced? I want to taunt him with that thin line he plays with," Freyja said with her hands on her hips. Carla grinned with glee; Owen would be destroyed.

"The war is on," Athena said excitedly, tapping the bottom end of her spear on the floor a few times.

"You never mind what the rest of us will be up to. But, our little witch, you will be the conjurer. We'll need you to chant these incantations," Shiva said and produced, as if from an invisible pocket, a scroll that was probably as old as Earth itself. He went to hand it to Carla but stopped to clarify what it was they were all offering: Carla would invoke the powers and hold the vision of all who would get their comeuppance, the gods would do their work, and once her offenders had been ruined and the town a mess, they would bring Ocean back immediately so that she could be with her love again. At this point Carla added in her mind the image of herself and Ocean skipping off to wherever their hearts desired – perhaps Germany, perhaps Peru. And when she died, she would spend eternity with the deities, no matter what. Carla was more than happy with the way that sounded.

The usual suspects were down at the Red Oak and the deities would find it easy to spark the fire there. Nicholas was fast asleep at home, having gone to bed feeling bad about letting Carla go from the antique shop. His wife, Beth, was having her evening drink with the others at the pub, and Nicholas had no idea where Lawrence had gone. Freyja was delighted to find Owen sitting in the corner of the pub with half a glass of Carling and fiddling with his phone. He was pretending to answer messages, but he was actually keeping one eye on Rachel, whose breasts jiggled in her black scoop-neck top as she wiped the bar. Freyja sauntered over to the bar and waited for Rachel to notice her. Rachel met Freyja's eyes and took a step back from the beauty that thrust itself before her. "A glass of your best red, please," Freyja requested, and twirled her ponytail with her head cocked to one side. Rachel asked her to present some ID. Freyja pretended to be startled by the question. She looked around her, in particular at Owen, hoping to catch his attention, and loudly responded that she was of age. Owen, hearing Rachel insist on seeing some ID or else Freyja would have to leave, stepped up to rescue Freyja from the embarrassment. Owen actually just wanted to introduce himself to the sexy, young woman he'd never seen before. "Don't you go to my college?" he said to Freyja. "I'm sure I've seen you in the halls. Rachel, this girl is no younger than you. Pour her a glass, would you?" Owen held out a hand to shake Freyja's.

"I am studying at the moment," Freyja said, going along with the lie. "Thank you for recognising me. You're Mr Reeves, aren't you?" She was excellent at getting her eyes to sparkle, to get the smile just right – a smile that suggested he imagine what her lips could do.

"I am indeed," Owen replied, a little baffled as to how she actually did know his name. "Please call me Owen," he continued, now not only attracted to her, but excited by her, too.

"Anthropology," Freyja told Rachel, who was now reaching for a wine glass. "That's what I'm studying." Rachel rolled her eyes and thought she'd love to spit in this girl's drink as well, but now that she'd been caught doing it, she couldn't risk losing her job. Instead, she mouthed curses and insults to the bottle she was pouring from. As she slammed the drink on the bar and told Freyja how much it cost, Rachel could see from a sideways glance that Owen was getting flustered. He was blushing and digging his hands into his jeans' pocket to pay for the girl's drink.

Now Rachel had not only lost the boy she desired, but she was also losing the interest of the man that desired her. She was seething, and this was Chang'e's cue to up the ante on the forces that take hold of the emotions. By the clock tower in the square, the Chinese goddess was drawing down the power of the moon. Soon those with frazzled nerves and high blood pressure would be losing their minds. At the same time, Carla was chanting Sally's name into the incantation. The wildness of the night and the storm that was growing more vicious with every minute would make great weather for the bubbling pot to overspill.

It was coming up to ten-thirty and the rain was whipping at Sally's windows. She was sitting on the sofa biting her nails. Every now and again, a thunderbolt would make her shiver and she was growing more anxious with the need to have Jeremy in bed with her – especially on a night like this. It had been so long since she had felt his body between her thighs and had crawled her fingers through his hairy chest – the way he throbbed with every pant as he lay beneath her. She was contemplating going to see him. He'd said they'd never do it again, but on a wild night like this, how could one withstand not having someone to cling to? Without someone to touch, to soothe one's galloping heart, set into motion by the lightning, the lashes of rain and wind. Sally bounced her knees up and down, fighting the urges in her mind and body.

Mercury was on the other side of the room watching her, enjoying his work while remaining invisible – another wonderful power to possess. He was tricking Sally's heart into needing Jeremy; he was stirring the desires within her. He was imagining the yearning as lava in her veins pumping, burning, and gurgling up to the surface. It didn't take long before she was grabbing her house keys and coat, and power-walking her way over to number twenty-two of Honeysuckle Road.

Raijin struck a tree just outside of the pub, which landed on the bar manager's car, causing a chilling crunch before the car's alarm pierced through the air. "What the hell was that?" Beth, who had been having her well-earned Chardonnay, jumped up from her seat and looked out the window. "Ken, your car! Your car's been hit." Ken ran over to check the damage. There were gasps from some people and a few laughs from others, but they all soon became concerned with the fury of the weather and wondered if their own cars would be all right.

"I don't like the look of that storm, Ken. What if none of us can get home?" Carol piped up.

"You're only open for another hour, Carol, let us have another one," a rather drunk Peter Biggins yelled from his spot by the cigarette machine. Ken, furious about his car, decided that the laughs and cheers were over and told Carol to close up. Everyone was to go home because the storm was getting unpredictable.

"How are you getting home?" Owen asked Freyja, and then apologised for not having asked her name.

"It's Isabelle," she told him. She'd always liked that name. "And I'll walk, thanks." She smiled and, as she looked away, Owen ran his eyes up her legs, wondering what they looked like under those tights.

"I can't have you walking home in that weather. Can I

accompany you? I'd feel terrible if anything were to happen to you." Freyja placed a hand on his arm and told him how sweet that was, and how about the lovely bar girl? Wouldn't she feel safer walking with the two of them also? Owen couldn't get his answer in before Freyja called over to Rachel saying that they'd walk each other home in a group and that she must join them.

"That's OK, I've got my mum to walk home with," Rachel said. Owen showed his delight at her refusal a little too much, Rachel saw it and it made her feel like taunting him. "Actually, you're right. We should all walk together. With all those trees coming down, we could look out for one another."

The four of them set off for Honeysuckle Road. Owen insisted that Carol and Rachel be dropped off first and that it made sense for Isabelle to wait out the weather back at his place, which was only a road away from theirs. They were soaked to the bone from the rain and it was hard to see through it. Carol pulled her scarf tightly over herself; Freyja let her coat flap open and her dress flutter above her thighs. Owen was walking behind them. When lightning struck again, Freyja grabbed Rachel and pulled her close. "It's frightening, isn't it? Makes you want to get all snuggly with someone." Rachel was slightly taken aback by the sudden body contact, but she let Freyja hold onto her anyway, while Owen wildly fantasised about the two of them in an embrace.

Back at the Abbott residence, Athena was stirring the air with warfare. She was setting the grounds for battle. Shiva would be stepping onto the stage in the final act of this show, and when Carla reached her crescendo of chanting, that would be his cue. Shiva took great pleasure in his ability to create, but his true glory was his ability to destroy. He summoned the almighty forces that could take away life. He held his trident with both hands and focused on Carla, who spoke the Sanskrit words with impressive ease. His eyes lit up with gold as the skies rumbled heavier now than before.

On the other side of Carol's front door, Jeremy had surrendered to Sally's pleas and had allowed her to take him into her hungry mouth. In the hallway she clutched at his chest while on her knees. Athena could feel the thunder horses charging across the sky to rile up the anger and hatred that was caught in the air below them. Raijin stirred the floods. The surrounding marshy lands folded under the overflowing river on the edge of the town, and the flood would eventually spill out down the roads that encircled them all. No one would be going anywhere.

Carol unlocked the door, pushed it open and screamed at what she saw, her keys flying through the air and landing in the terracotta plant pot by the door where they sank in the rainwater it held. Sally jumped up and hit herself against the staircase. Her lipstick was smeared across one side of her face, and Rachel screamed at the sight of her father's erect penis. Owen let out a nervous laugh, and Freyja held a hand to her mouth in shock, but was actually trying to stop the delight from escaping her lips. Athena pulled the pin from the grenade that was Carol's heart and the explosion that came caused all to leap away and shield their faces. Fists pounded at Jeremy first, before Carol got to Sally's hair, which came out in clumps as she bashed her head against the banister. Jeremy was trying to pull his pants up but was shaking too much to get a proper hold of the zip. Owen stepped back from the fight and told Rachel that he and Isabelle should get going. "Don't you dare leave me with this! What am I supposed to do?" Rachel was crying now, her hands reaching out to stop her mother but just as quickly retreating. Jeremy attempted to pull Carol off Sally, but was punched in the ear. Rachel begged Owen to take her back to his place so that she could get away from all this.

Owen shook his head and started to walk out the door with Freyja's wrist in his hand when the tree by the downstairs window was struck by lightning, blasting the panes. Glass shattered all over Owen, who fell to the floor. His phone skidded across the stone path and before it got wet, Jeremy picked it up. This is where Mercury's trickery got really creative: the phone "malfunctioned" and brought up text messages on the screen that had been sent between Owen and Rachel. Jeremy's head was spinning but he still managed to catch lines that said things like "I'm rock hard now" and Rachel's reply of "You look good." And then there were a few flashes of photographs: Owen's stomach, a peppering of pubic hair and a final caption that said: "Let me know when you want to see more."

No one heard the crack of the phone against Owen's head because of the cacophony of rain, screams, crying, thunder, and the destruction that was falling down around them. Shiva saw the shard of glass go right through Owen's jacket and into his stomach and knew that it was time to start reaping souls.

Carla could feel that it was working. All the while she was chanting, she felt surges of electricity run through her body. She stood up after she'd finished and drank some wine as she waited for the deities to return. She was vibrating slightly, even though she essentially felt numb, like guitar strings that are no longer being plucked but are still humming. She sank into the sofa, turning over in her mind how Ocean would look when he was brought back to her. Just then, there was banging at her front door. There was no way that the deities would be knocking; surely they'd just appear. Then she heard the familiar voice of Lawrence calling her name. "Carla, please! I need to speak to you!" He was begging and banging and Carla wasn't sure whether his desperation was based on him needing her, or because of the weather. She set her glass down quietly and walked silently towards the door. "Let me in, Carla!" But as soon as her hand reached for the lock, Shiva appeared behind her.

"Let's not complicate things, shall we? I'll send him away. It's almost time for us to finish up and go. He'll only be a bother." Shiva pointed his trident to the door and Lawrence was soon apologising for disturbing her, and then he was gone.

"What did he want?" Carla asked the god.

"He thinks he's falling in love with you and wants to abandon his family and this town to be with you," Shiva explained. Carla exhaled with relief that Shiva had sent him away. He was right, that would have been a bother. "He'll get over it very quickly." Carla asked Shiva how everything was going. He sat up straight, adjusted himself in his seat and began to gleefully explain it all.

"Rachel and Owen are no longer of this world," Shiva explained, recounting that the finale of the night saw Rachel grabbing her father's car keys to try and get Owen to a hospital because she couldn't get through to the emergency services on the phone. Rachel however couldn't see through the heavy rain and, on their way out of town, swerved the car to avoid a falling tree. The car skidded, clipped another car, and span until the vehicle landed in the flood. Owen's spirit had left his body just before the impact. Carol couldn't stop beating Sally, who eventually let go and passed over into the spirit realm also. Jeremy had been chased out of the house by his guilt some ten minutes before. He would make it to Nicholas's house, where he'd be put up for the night until the truth about his indiscretions would cast him out of town for good some days later. The police would arrive in the morning to arrest Carol for manslaughter. Freyja meanwhile had taken leave of the situation and joined Shiva and Carla back at the cottage and waited for the others

Mercury returned next. The storm calmed down when Raijin appeared, and Chang'e hushed the moon in order to settle everyone's emotions. Athena concluded that the battle had been won. They were all together again and Carla would finally receive her beloved Ocean and leave Red Oak forever. "Are you ready for him?" Freyja asked. She was back in her long gown, her hair loose and bountiful once again. Carla nodded.

"Close your eyes, Carla," Chang'e said, a smile on her lips like someone about to reveal a wonderful surprise. Carla felt another presence in the room and grinned before she opened her eyes again. There stood Ocean as beautiful as she remembered him. But his eyes were wet and his skin was pale and the cuffs of his jumper sleeves were torn.

"Ocean," Carla whispered. She took a closer look at the two vertical slits on his wrists. "Ocean, what have you done? What's happening? What is this?" Carla looked around at the gods and goddesses for the answers that Ocean wouldn't speak.

"He's dead, Carla," Athena said, and stood by Carla's side. She set her shield down and placed one arm around Carla, while the other still held her spear. "And if you want to have him forever, you have to be too." Athena took her spear and stabbed it into Carla's heart.

Carla wailed but soon went silent. She looked at the crimson liquid spreading across her chest and down her clothes. "We'll take you both now," Shiva said and stroked Carla's head, hushing into her ear to soothe her. She collapsed in his arms and he laid her down on the floor. When Carla's soul left her body, it stood up and went to embrace Ocean.

"We're together now, just like we wanted," Ocean said to her and pressed his ghostly lips against hers. "Nothing can stop us anymore." Carla looked down at her body; the blood was now staining the carpet beneath.

"You tricked me, all of you. You never told me he was dead, you never told me I'd have to—" Carla began to sob, thinking of all the things she'd never get to do, about the life she wouldn't be able to live. She felt a sudden need to hold her parents again. She would have talked to her father more and would have undone her two years of silence. She saw her mother's tears, Victoria upset at her ruined birthday party, Jason spraining his wrist when he fell over Carla's foot. She felt the need to go back and do it all differently. She would have never let Ocean go the first time and she would never have come to Red Oak.

"Isn't it better this way?" Mercury consoled her. "Now you can be with your soulmate, travel the world like we do, and never have to feel the pain and suffering that your body did when alive." The deities formed a circle around Carla and Ocean.

"Time to go now," Raijin said. "Our glorious kingdom is waiting."

Morgana's Shadow

IT WAS MORGANA who Joshua said he saw me kiss; it was a kiss to seal a deal. She said she'd give me wings, make me a shape-shifter, and give me the ability to not be me whenever I wanted. It was Morgana who appeared to me, springing out from behind the tree I was resting under. She moved like a leaf in the breeze to greet me, her long black hair down to her elbows. It was she who asked if I dared pluck the sacred flower, and I stammered to answer; I had been startled by her invasion. But I was brought up to never tell lies. It's one of the Ten Commandments, and my mother read them to me again once I was back at home, dragged there by the wrist under Joshua's angry hand. I always knew when she was about to read from the Great Book because she'd look to the air above my head and not into my eyes, as if she were receiving direction from somewhere up there. She'd nod and take her small red cloth-bound bible, frayed at its edges, from the pocket of her thick-knit brown cardigan, and purse her lips as she searched for the right verse. Joshua said the word "filth" when he explained the incident, as I tried not to let my body melt into what Morgana had made me. I could feel the change in me after that kiss; what was once solid in me was now malleable, and it could be moulded into another being, another me.

I wanted to tell them it was magic, but I didn't know what the harshest condemnation would be: admitting to dabbling in witchcraft, or being forced to announce that I liked girls and therefore needed to be put right. Either way, they were going to put me right. When Joshua called my name from the clearing in the woods, Morgana backed away out of his sight, behind that same tree, and then she was gone. The flower I'd plucked, the sacred bloom belonging to her, turned to black and crumbled in my hand as if it had been tossed into a flame. The rich, purple, silky beauty of it was now dead in my palm. I felt instantly nauseous then, and that's why I believed her. Something had entered me – or rather, had awakened in me – and in the pit of my gut I no longer felt human. A watery feeling rippled through me. I know I hadn't dreamt it all; it hadn't been a reverie, proven real by Joshua being a witness to the Great Morgana standing there. But him seeing it had also been my doom. My brother ran to me, as if he was hoping for a confrontation with the woman who had turned his sister, who had corrupted her with her filthy whore lips. But when he'd seen that she was no longer there, his venom turned on me. How funny for him to call me a snake all the way home – he was the one hissing and spitting as he dragged me along.

I am not a snake, I am now a bird; I have wings. They are there somewhere inside me, I can feel them. I haven't yet sprouted them, but I know Morgana gave them to me. I plucked the sacred flower and Morgana said that turning me was punishment for doing so, but perhaps it is also a gift. I can turn into a bird when I want to and fly away. I'm just not yet quite sure how; perhaps if I concentrate. There isn't much I can look at here in the guest bedroom besides the crucifix in front of me on the bare white wall. Jesus is not even nailed to it; there is no ally to look at in joint suffering, just a plain wooden shape with no embellishments. I cannot see much else.

My mother and Joshua, and even my father when he came home, made sure to strap me in good and tight. Dad came back from work and had walked straight into Mum and Joshua's discussion about the abomination of having a lesbian in the family, and what's more, a harlot one who would kiss a strange older woman in the woods. Mum raised her voice, but there was nothing coming from my father: he was silent when he was most angry. That voiceless air around him is constricting, as if he is purposefully suffocating you with it using his mind. He won't say anything when the belt is snapped free from around his trousers and wound up in his hands. The loose end is the buckle side, which he will whip once or twice against the air before it hits my skin. He won't say anything afterwards either, when he threads it back through the loops and fastens it around him, leaving me holding in my tears until my lips shake uncontrollably, riding the wave of the sting on the tops of my thighs. I'd rather he spoke, like Joshua and Mum. I'd rather he screamed accusations like they always did, than say nothing at all.

I didn't get the belt when he came in today. He is even angrier than that. Just pure silence; he is pondering a greater punishment. My forehead is wet from where holy water was flicked on me. Mum stood over the bed, holding the Virgin Mary bottle she brought back from Lourdes. Joshua told me that I'd be going to hell if I didn't stop being dirty. I wanted to explain that I had just been to heaven. I had been in the woods where the sunlight streamed down on all the glorious creatures that came up from the ground, rejoicing up to the sky: the bluebells, the rich green grass, the mushrooms, the moss – everything that was created by Him, glowing, just for me.

The air was soft and lazy there, perfect for a late spring day. The perfume of sun-soaked flowers and grass gently drifted around me, like incense burning quietly in church. I usually walk fast through the woods whenever I go there, more for the routine of exercise than anything else, but today I decided to sit down and take in the beauty. I sat cross-legged against the tree and watched a white butterfly skim across the plants and then I looked back down at the ladybird climbing my shoe – and that's when I saw it at the corner of my eye. One single purple flower, a flower so vivid and so unique I'd never seen anything like it before. I saw it as a gesture from God, a present given to me in thanks for taking the time to sit and absorb the wonder He had created. I wrapped my fingers around the stem and pulled at it, wanting to keep this token of heaven. And that's when she appeared.

"You'll have to pay the price for that, my child," Morgana had said.

"I'm sorry, I didn't realise I couldn't take the flower. I know it is sacred. I know, that's why I thought it was so beautiful," I said quickly, used to giving an explanation for everything.

Morgana straightened herself up. She was tall, but from where I was sitting under that tree, she may as well have been a tower. Her shadow darkened the land around us. "You just take whatever you want, do you? But you're not used to being given what you don't want, are you?" she challenged me; her eyes seemed to be of some unearthly colour, violet or lilac.

I objected to what she said; it wasn't true at all. Everyone was given things they didn't want, including me. "I didn't mean to upset you," I said, still not knowing who she was or why she had appeared like this. She then announced herself as Morgana, the great Fey Queen, and showed me her magic. She turned into a deer and bowed her head, antlers pointed at me. She nudged me in the shoulder and I rolled over a little, losing my balance. Was she the devil my family talked about so much? I couldn't speak, I was so terrified. Would anyone believe me if I told them this? Quickly enough, her body shifted back into the tall, dark-haired woman. She leant forward and stroked my cheek with one finger; I stiffened at her touch and closed my eyes. Perhaps if I said the Lord's Prayer, I'd be saved.

There was silence then, and I opened my eyes to check it hadn't been a hallucination. But she was still there, studying me, her head cocked to one side. She was leaning on the trunk of the tree. I stood up slowly. "You poor darling girl," she said, and in a rather sweet tone, to my surprise. "I like you. What's your name, dear one?" I was afraid to look at the brewing storm in her eyes, but I turned to her anyway; the colour in them had changed, they were now hazel.

"Marie-Claire," I breathed.

"Marie-Claire, I'm going to give you something. It'll be something that you want, but you don't know it yet. But careful, it is still a curse."

I shook my head. There wasn't anything I wanted except to be left alone. And then it occurred to me: I didn't want to just be left alone by this strange woman; I wanted to be left alone by everybody. I watched her shift into a bird of prey, a hawk. Her wings were layered with the most beautiful feathers; they spread out far and wide and shaded me from the sunlight when she hovered in the air. Amber eyes were now fixed on me. "This is what you'll be," I heard her voice say, but no words came from the hawk's beak. She then let out a cry and it was the sound of freedom. That's the only way I could interpret it, from the way it rang through me. I accepted her spell, which she said must be sealed with a kiss. It was then Joshua who took my freedom away.

I doze for a while, drowsy from insults, holy water, and confinement. If only I could learn how to get my wings like Morgana did. Perhaps I could turn into a deer, too, or any other animal I could imagine. But a bird – yes, a bird would be perfect for now. I try to picture myself as a hawk, but I soon drop away from the conscious world.

"Sick, dear Lord, sick to her very core, diseased and stained with the foulest lust." I wake up to my mother's voice and the thick smell of misery. The room hasn't been aired; the windows are shut and have been for some time. I can smell my own contained sleep-breath and bed-ridden odours. Mother is talking into her book, the only book she accepts as existing. She is sitting in one of the chairs taken from the kitchen table; her feet are resting on the frame of the bed. Every bit of her is covered, right up to the neck, in a long skirt and a polo neck. Only her frowning face and her anxious hands are bare; she is clutching her set of rosary beads. When she sees that my eyes are open she looks back down into her lap and continues to mutter her hurtful words. Until I find my voice to speak she ignores me. My throat feels swollen.

"I wasn't being lustful," I say, but it doesn't sound like words, just tones that sound like they are drowning. But her

look tells me that she understood what was said. She is thinking about my words and examining my face. She then puts her
rosary beads on the bedside table and picks up a cup of tea.

"You need to drink this, Marie-Claire." My brain tells me
to sit up but my body does not move; I am still tied to the
bed.

"How can I?" I croak. She sighs through her nostrils, sets
the cup back down, and loosens the rags she used to restrain
me. Restrain me from what, though, I am not sure; I will not
scream or hit her. When my hands are free, I rotate my wrists
and bones click and crunch. I gingerly sit up and wriggle
against the pillow. I take my tea, and for just a moment, this
scenario is innocent: my mother giving me a cup of tea while
I am weak in bed; her just sitting there, watching over me.

"Won't be long now until you're purged of it, Marie-Claire.
Until it is all gone from your system." I shut my ears off to the
rest of what she has to say. Outside the bedroom door, I can
hear the TV being switched on. Loud cartoon music fills the
quiet for a few seconds until it is turned down. Joshua. Even
at sixteen, he still enjoys watching juvenile nonsense. I am
wriggling my toes as I sip on the tea that I can't quite taste;
something about my feet feels odd. They feel thin and barely
there. I flex my foot and my nails scratch against the mattress.
But how can they? They're not long or sharp. I do it again and
get the same sensation. I rub one foot against the other and
have to stifle my gasp when I feel claws where toes should be.

There is a knock on the door and I freeze. "Bernadette, he's
here," my father's muffled voice says formally.

"Give me two minutes, Michael, thank you," Mum replies,
and adjusts her clothes, making sure her jumper isn't riding

up and her skirt isn't slipping down. "You need to finish that tea. Now." I gulp down the rest of it, wincing at its cold temperature. "Good," she whispers, as if cooing a baby. She takes the cup and my stomach turns over. I feel weak again. The drowsiness comes quickly. The bedroom door opens, and I hear my father and mother by the door. Then a third person comes in. "Thank you so much for coming, Father," says my mum, and Morgana comes to me again, but this time, in the blackness.

She puts her forehead to mine and with that touch I am suddenly transported to a hilltop at night. I am gazing at the moon; it is impossibly large and delicious to look at. Its texture seems buttery, as if cream has been poured into it. Morgana appears next to me and smiles a devious smile before she shifts into a wolf. Her long flowing clothes drop to the floor and there she is panting gleefully, her eyes flickering like coins caught in sunlight. "Make it so," her voice says in my head, and she gazes into my eyes before bolting across the hill into the dark, dense forest to my left. I stand up and watch her disappear before I hear her howling. I want to howl too and so I do, and as that sound reverberates in my body, I am suddenly on four legs. I look down: I have paws and I have claws. My ears are tall and keen, my sight is sharp, and my sense of smell is wide open. I am taking in the scent of night-bloom flowers wafting over from the forest, the damp bark of the trees, and the trail of Morgana. I take off and run. I run so fast I hear the air whipping past me. I am exhilarated, I am moving in a way that could never be known to a human. I love what I am suddenly capable of. I am in love with this feeling; I am in love with me.

I open one eye slowly and carefully to a lamp-lit bedroom. I am still in the spare room. I bet they won't let me go back to my room until it has been fully searched for sinful paraphernalia. It is evening; I can see the darkness out the window. I have no idea how many hours have lapsed. I have no idea where I have just been. Wasn't I with the Fey Queen, racing through a forest? I am wondering now what was in that tea. The priest enters the room again, this time alone. I quickly close my eyes before he looks at me. Perhaps he has just taken a short biscuit break with my mother. She loves to entertain men of the cloth; she'll bring out her best plates, apply some lipstick, and spray herself with a horribly synthetic perfume that gives me a headache.

I hear the priest open the window; I thank him for it silently. "Blessed Lord, it has been asked of me by this loving family . . ." his steady voice begins. A ringing in my ears abrasively interrupts my ability to listen to him. I feel my body jolt from the noise, but I am sure the priest thinks that the demon in me is responding to his exorcism. A pain comes with the high-pitched ringing in my ears; a pain that is eating its way through my legs. It feels like my tendons and veins are being gnawed at. I cry out and the priest raises his voice, but I still can't hear him. The lower half of my body is turning, I am turning, I feel my talons kicking at the sheets and my feathers pushing through the skin at the tops of my thighs, the pain of them ripping through me. I clutch the sheets with both hands, fastened down on either side of me; Mum must have tied the restraints around my wrists again when I drifted off. The fright of all this makes me focus on being me again. I want to be Marie-Claire. And with that thought, my gut twists and

I abruptly and violently vomit all over one side of my pillow. The ringing has stopped. I can feel my human legs again. The priest hushes me in a kind tone and then leaves the room to find someone who will clean up my sick.

I am still drowsy when my mother bursts into the room with a cloth and some disinfectant. I can smell it the minute she takes the cap off. I am drained from all the energy I used to attempt my shape-shift, and so all I can do is roll over away from the vomit and let her clean it up. The rags have no give on my right wrist, so my arm remains behind me.

"It's all done now, Bernadette. She should be feeling better soon," the priest says delicately, his voice sounding so far away. My mother stops wiping the pillow to thank him.

"God bless you, Father. I am eternally grateful." I've never heard her sound so sweet. She goes to see him out the front door; I hear more thanks and praise echoing in the corridor. When the door clicks shut, she does not come back to remove the sheets. She doesn't come back at all. I roll back over to get comfortable, but the disinfectant sitting on top of the stench of vomit stings my eyes and nostrils. I look up at the window and realise that they have forgotten to close it again.

The house is eerily quiet for what feels like hours, but perhaps only half an hour has passed. I see the round doorknob turn and a gentle push is given. I see Joshua's thick brown hair before I see his face. We make eye contact for the first time in a long while; it is uncomfortable for me to look at him now. "You must be better now. Mum said you've purged." I do not answer him, but watch him step in a foot or two and shut the door behind him. He is in his bedclothes now, blue and grey tartan pyjama bottoms and a white T-shirt, a size too big for him. He sits on the edge of the bed and puts his hand on top of mine; it gives me the same sensation that a spider does when it walks along my skin. "Do you feel different?" he asks, stroking my hand now.

"Yes," I reply, my throat dry and hoarse.

"Shall we test it then? To see if you don't like girls anymore." I am frightened by what he might mean. His hand slides quickly from my hand and up to my breast and I cry out for him to get off me. He stops any sound from me by sticking his pointy, wet tongue in my mouth. He grabs the back of my hair and pushes my head to him so he can thrust his tongue in deeper. I want to gag. My scream is muffled and I can't push him off while my hands are tied, but I wriggle and yank my wrists with all the strength I have left in me. Finally, his tongue retracts enough for me to bite it and he growls and pulls away.

The palm of his hand slaps a sting so strong across my cheek that my whole face vibrates. He comes in again for an attack, this time with both hands around my neck. This is it; it's going to happen now. The ringing in my ears is back. Morgana's eyes flicker in my mind's eye. I concentrate hard. I feel the hawk. I am the hawk.

I rip myself free from the rags and my large wing bats Joshua away from me. I fly at him, threatening to scratch his face with my talons. He is petrified and shouts for Mum and Dad. I test out my new lungs and a loud cry sweeps across the room with my breath – the sound of freedom. I leave Joshua alone and make my exit through the open window and out into the night.

I circle the roof of the house and soar up higher and higher, taking pleasure in watching it shrink smaller and smaller. The bliss, this sweet, delectable bliss of flying has me laughing inside. I fly away back to the forest where heaven once lay, where I plucked the most sacred flower in existence, where I found the all-magical Queen of the Fey. I want to find her again and ask her to show me what other creatures I could be.

Acknowledgements

DEEPEST GRATITUDE GOES to Norman Thompson, the greatest supporter, listener and partner, to my first ever mentor Catherine Schikkerling, to Marisa Henderson, Joe Butler, Katherine Cross, to the women in my family: my grandmother, mother, and my sister and comrade, Cindy Marie-Jeanne.

Warmest thanks to my professional mentor Courttia Newland and The Almasi League Writers Programme, to Ellah Allfrey, Jaclyn Arndt, Spread the Word and The WoMentoring Project.

Special thanks to my agent, Elise Dillsworth.

This book has been typeset by
SALT PUBLISHING LIMITED
using Neacademia, a font designed by Sergei Egorov
for the Rosetta Type Foundry in the Czech Republic.
It is manufactured using Creamy 70gsm, a Forest
Stewardship Council™ certified paper from Stora Enso's
Anjala Mill in Finland. It was printed and bound by
Clays Limited in Bungay, Suffolk, Great Britain.

CROMER, NORFOLK
GREAT BRITAIN
MMXVI